BOOMERANG LIES

A NOVEL

Barbara Wood Palak

BOOMERANG LIES

A NOVEL

BARBARA WOOD POLAK

Boomerang Lies is a product of the author's imagination and is used fictitiously, and, except in the case of historical fact, any resemblance to actual persons, living or dead, is purely coincidental.

Published by Four Cats Publishing, LLC

No portion of this book may be copied or reproduced by any means without the expressed, written consent of the author.

Copyright © 2014 by BARBARA Wood Polak

All rights reserved.

Cover design by Tonya Foreman. Cover photos by Steve Foreman (buildings) and Ryan Foreman (snow landscape).

Author photograph by Stephanie DiFiore
Dog photograph by Barbara Wood Polak

Printed in the United States

ISBN-10: 0988839954
ISBN-13: 978-0-9888399-5-3

To my loving family. I love you all.

Lots of people want to ride with you in the limo, but what you want is someone who will take the bus with you when the limo breaks down.

—Oprah Winfrey

The game of life is a game of boomerangs. Our thoughts, deeds, and words return to us sooner or later with astounding accuracy.

—Florence Scovel Shinn (1871-1940)

Acknowledgments

I want to thank my family and friends for encouraging me throughout the process of writing *Boomerang Lies*. Thanks to my husband for all his computer help and thanks to Four Cats Publishing, LLC, for making publishing this book so easy.

Chapter 1

August 27

It was one of those hot summer days at the end of August, and the temperature must have been at least 90 degrees. Chris pulled the green rusty truck into the closest parking space she could find. The rental truck was hot and humid and, of course, had no air conditioning. As she looked around this unfamiliar and intimidating neighborhood, she was filled with dread of her task at hand. This compound was so completely different from anything she had ever experienced before. All she saw were rows and rows of large apartment buildings as far as the eye could see. Most were in desperate need of repair, and more than a few had boarded windows with blackened burned out areas that looked like a painter had gone wild with black paint.

Here, there were no one-family houses, no well-cared-for sweeping green lawns, no towering trees, and no sense of peace and safety. Grass was nonexistent, only weeds growing up here and there through the dry, caked soil and broken sidewalks. The absence of trees, shrubs, and flowers added to the forlorn appearance of the compound. But the thing that made the biggest impact on Chris and scared her the most was the many people, mostly men, just sitting on benches, stumps, or the ground, and some just standing around. She had felt several pairs of eyes on her yesterday when she unloaded the truck the first time, and it made her feel very uneasy.

As she rolled up the windows and stepped down from the truck, she knew that she couldn't show her fear; she had to be strong for her children. She reminded herself that this was temporary, just until she could find a way to get them all out of this situation. She repeated the word temporary in her mind and prayed that it would be so.

So with feigned courage Chris started her task for today: unloading boxes and small pieces of furniture up to the fourth floor of Building Number Six in Willshire Development.

At least, so far, the rickety elevator was working fairly well today. Yesterday, she had wasted over an hour waiting for the elevator when she moved kitchen boxes. For the next three hours, she moved her things from the truck, up the stairs of the building, into the elevator, to the apartment over and over again. This ritual was so tiring, but finally only one item was left.

Chris swore silently as she tried to push the wingback chair through the narrow doorway. The metal strip at the threshold of the door caught the chair by one of its wooden legs. The metal won, making a sickening groaning noise as it partially ripped the leg from the chair's frame. When the chair finally cleared the door, Chris bent the leg back into place and plopped down on its soft wine-colored cushion. Feeling totally exhausted, hot, sweaty, and so utterly alone in this endeavor, she pressed her face into the familiar fabric and let the tears fall.

She had been fighting tears all day. But now sitting in this hot, dingy, wretched place she couldn't hold back any longer. She needed to cry, hoping to find some relief from the lead ball that lay in the pit of her stomach and the shaky, forlorn feeling that came from a place where her peaceful heart used to be.

She sat for what seemed like forever, feeling sorry for herself, and calling herself a fool for thinking that she could handle this move by herself. Chris always did what she had to do to get things done. But at this moment her confidence was waning, and she would have gratefully let anyone lend a hand. Unfortunately, no hands were available except her own. Both hands felt stiff, and the muscles in her arms were sore. She stretched her aching arms toward the ceiling hoping to find some relief. Glancing up at her hands, Chris was startled by what she saw. They were both grimy, and her once always-manicured nails were dirty, chipped, and torn. One of her fingers had a slight cut on the knuckle, and a thin line of blood had dried a rusty brown.

She also noticed that there was still an indentation on her left ring finger where her wedding rings had resided for seventeen years. At first, she felt almost naked without the rings, and at times when she was nervous or bored, her thumb would reach over to twirl the rings, as it had thousands of times before, only to find nothing to twirl. Her heart would leap, but only for a second, until she remembered.

She sat in the chair for five minutes or so, and with great reluctance, grabbed the arms of the chair and slowly stood up. Crying time was over. It had to be over; there was too much to do. Once out of the chair, she pushed it to the room that would serve as the living room. On the ugly green almost threadbare carpet in that room lie the fruits of her day's labor. There were six boxes, three lamps, a coffee table, two end tables, and a small bookshelf. It didn't look like much, but it was the best she could do.

Chris recalled happier moves made with her family in the past. That was when Ted, her husband, actually her soon to be ex-husband, had been employed by Billingly Brokerage Firm. It had been so easy. Movers came in and packed, moved, and unpacked. The movers brought their own boxes and wrapping material and cleaned up the mess after the move. That was it! But that life was in the past. The present held no conveniences for her now. At least she had been able to find a man and his son to move the larger pieces of furniture tomorrow. The price was very reasonable and that was of utmost importance.

Looking at her watch, she realized that she only had three hours until the kids got home from an outing with the neighbors. She got out her cleaning supplies and did the best she could scrubbing the bathroom and kitchen, vacuuming, dusting, and mopping the other rooms. The only room that had carpet was the living room, and it was badly in need of shampooing, but that would have to wait. The other rooms had floors of either faded linoleum or scratched wood.

Despite her efforts, the apartment continued to look sad and unwelcome. It had the odor of someone unsuccessfully trying to cover up a worn, dusty smell with a few sprays of disinfectant. Even with the windows wide open, the heat was intense, and Chris had to stop and sit down. She rested for a few moments and thanked God that summer would soon be over. There would be no air conditioning here, but hopefully they wouldn't be stuck here next summer.

Chris decided to start unpacking some of the boxes in the kitchen area. The brown-colored moving boxes just about covered the tiny kitchen floor. Stepping gingerly around and over the boxes, she opened the small kitchen window over the sink as wide as it would go. Sliding a few boxes aside, she cleared a small area and knelt down to start unpacking.

In the second box, she found the glasses and mugs. Chris smiled when she unwrapped a large mug with a big smiling sunflower, a birthday gift from her neighbor Laura. She clutched this bright, cheery mug remembering all the good times she and Laura had shared over the last seven years. They had become best friends, and whenever either needed to borrow an onion or egg, or maybe just someone to talk to, there were only two driveways separating them.

Thinking about Laura, Chris felt a strong longing to be home. She put down the mug and almost tripped over the boxes in her rush to leave. Quickly she closed the windows, grabbed her purse and keys from the chipped and permanently stained countertop, opened the door, and stepped into the hall. She felt such a sense of relief to be leaving this alien place. Right now she needed to go home, to the place that had been her home for the last seven years.

As she turned to lock the door, she noticed a woman standing in the doorway of the apartment next to hers. The woman was just standing there watching. They looked at each other for a brief time, and as Chris raised her hand to acknowledge the stranger, the dark-haired woman stepped back into her apartment and shut the door.

Why the action of a perfect stranger would have such an impact on Chris, she couldn't imagine. But she felt embarrassed and wounded. "I hate you," she whispered. "I hate this place. I hate this building," and she felt a real need to add, "I'm going home."

After one quick look at the dreaded elevator, Chris decided to take the stairs and heaved open the heavy door and descended the four flights of stairs as quickly as she could. Once out of the horrid apartment, Chris hurried to the parking area, located her rental truck, unlocked the door, and stepped up to sit in the driver's seat.

The green rusty truck started with a reluctant growl and rumbled through the strange streets until it came to the entrance of the highway. Chris drove for several miles until she spotted the sign for the turnoff for Ridgewood. It was amazing how her body seemed to relax at the simple thought of Ridgewood Heights. It had meant peace and happiness for seven years, until three months ago. That's when the nightmare had begun.

Was it only three months, she asked herself? It had seemed much longer than that. Actually, it had started earlier than three months, she just hadn't known.

Chapter 2

June 23, Two Months Earlier

It was a few minutes after six in the evening, and Chris had just finished showering, grabbed a fluffy white towel, quickly dried her body, and rubbed the towel briskly through her hair. She wrapped a mint-green terry cloth robe around her still-moist body and sat down at her dressing table to put on makeup and brush her hair.

She was excited for the first time in a long time. Her husband, Ted, had called from work this morning to tell her that he wanted to take her to Anton's for dinner and that he had something important to talk to her about. For the past several months, there had been definite signs that their marriage was going downhill. Ted had been working too much, hardly ever home for dinner, and when he was home all he did was grump around and make everyone miserable.

"Tonight," she thought, "I hope we can get everything resolved and be happy again. At least I'll know what is going on and that should be a relief."

Chris took extra time to carefully apply her makeup and brushed her shoulder-length auburn hair until it shone. She picked out an almost new teal scoop-neck dress that had scarf-like pieces attached at the waist to form a flowing skirt. The dress was made of silk and was one of her more daring purchases. She had worn it only one other time, eight months ago for their seventeenth wedding anniversary. Ted had said that she looked like dynamite. Well, she needed to look like dynamite again tonight.

The only jewelry Chris felt was needed was the diamond stud earrings that had belonged to her mother. She took them out of their box and carefully put them on. Stepping back, she looked into the mirror and liked what she saw. Ted used to tell her that she was his cute little redhead with bedroom eyes and sexy, full lips; he loved her freckles saying each one was a bonus feature. He used to gently take her face in his big hands and look into her green eyes saying, "Oh, Chris, this is the face of an angel, my angel," and then kiss her all over her face. He would say he was going to kiss every one of her freckles, and they would laugh and get silly and usually end up making love.

She had to smile at the memory of those times. Those times were gone now, and they hadn't had one of those times in months. She sure missed the fun and closeness and the intimacy that they had shared for so many years.

"Well, maybe tonight we can get to the bottom of this whole thing. Maybe, hopefully, we can get back what we had. Oh, please dear God, please, please, please. I want my husband back again like he was before. Before what, she wondered, what had happened? She had tried to figure that out so many times. Had she done something? Was Ted just tired of her or was there another woman? Oh God, please, not another woman, anything but not that."

Chapter 3

Chris' negative thoughts were interrupted by car doors slamming and the excited voices of her three children returning from an excursion with the next-door neighbors. Laura and Don Walker, their dear friends and neighbors, had two children, Jason and Patty. They were always going someplace fun and lately tried to include her children, Becky, Bobby, and Scott, in their activities.

Chris had to smile when she saw her brood come rambling into the kitchen, their happy faces glowing from humidity and contentment. Wittles, their little dog, a five-year old Bichon Frisé, came charging into the kitchen, frantically scampering about and wagging her tail at the arrival of the children. Scott, her youngest, sat down on the floor and grabbed Wittles and tried to calm her by petting her and letting her lick him on his face and neck.

He was the first to notice that Chris was all dressed up and looked up at her with his big green eyes and said, "Wow, Mom, you look really pretty." Then Becky asked where she was going and were they coming along. Chris told them about dinner with their father, and Bobby was relieved to hear that they weren't included in anything that involved dressing up. Once that was settled, they proceeded to tell Chris all about their trip to the Strawberry Festival: what they had to eat, what rides they went on, the funny things that happened, and how big, red, and juicy the strawberries were.

While they chattered on, Chris watched them and felt such a sense of pride that these little monkeys were her children. Becky, her oldest child, was fifteen. She was a beautiful slender girl with long reddish-brown hair and big green eyes. She was taller then Chris now at 5"4" and would be starting her second year in high school when summer was over. Bobby was twelve but was tall for his age and looked older. Everyone could tell that he was Ted's son because he had the same brown hair and brown eyes, and had Ted's mannerisms. Bobby would be in seventh grade this year, which meant he would go to a new school and leave elementary school for Junior High.

Scott was almost ten. His birthday, as he continually reminded everyone, was only a week away. Scott was still small in stature, but he had a big heart and a goofy grin that lit up his little freckled face whenever he smiled. How he got his blonde hair was anybody's guess, but he had Chris' green eyes and her disposition. Scott was not looking forward to the fall and being in fourth grade because he didn't care for school at all. Although he was smart enough and got good grades, Scott liked to be home with his family, friends, and dog.

Chris' thoughts were interrupted when Bobby declared that he was starving. Becky and Scott eagerly agreed with Bobby, and Chris made all three of them happy by ordering their favorite pizza and breadsticks with pizza sauce. When the food arrived, they ate like they had never seen food before and then went to the family room to watch TV.

It was nice to have a built-in babysitter, and Becky was very skillful and patient with her younger brothers, when she was being paid to babysit. Other times, she was a typical bossy big sister who thought her little brothers were a real pain.

Chris called Laura to see if she would be home for

the evening in case of an emergency. Laura said, "Not to worry," she would be home all evening. And then she added, "Chris, call me first thing in the morning and let me know what Ted has to say. I will be praying for you." Chris almost cried at her friend's concern but managed to keep control and told her that she would call as soon as she could.

It was almost eight o'clock before Ted came home. Chris saw the headlights roam down the long driveway as she watched through the kitchen window. Ted sat in the car for almost five minutes before he opened the door and slowly got out of the car. His steps to the kitchen door were slow and labored as if he were carrying a block of concrete. Watching Ted, she felt a chill go through her body. She knew something was terribly wrong, and suddenly she wished she could hide somewhere, wished they could postpone tonight. Maybe not knowing was better than what she feared he would say.

Chapter 4

Ted's thoughts were running rampant as he walked to the house. He knew he had only this one chance to get out of this mess and set things right. If Chris didn't believe him, he would be sunk. He needed her signature for the sale of the stocks and refinancing the house. If she wouldn't go along, well, she just had to go along, there was no other way. He had thought of forging her signature but that would only be as a last resort. Way too risky!

He went over his plan one last time. Be humble, act sincere, act penitent, act scared. Hell, acting scared would be easy: he was petrified. Chris had always gone along with what he wanted in the past. She trusted him and he had been able to reason with her or, if necessary, demand what he wanted, and she usually caved because she knew very little of their finances. But this was different. This was big. This was wrong, but he knew it was the only way.

Ted forced himself to put on a pitiful smile as he opened the door and greeted his wife. The kids were in the other room, thank God, so he didn't have to face them just yet. Chris looked nice and was apparently ready to leave for dinner. He thought this whole thing would be easier if she were a frumpy, lazy, uncaring wife, but she was none of these, and for a second he felt a sense of real guilt, but only for a second.

"Chris, I need a quick drink and then let's head out. Reservations are for 8:30." Then Ted figured he should add, "Chris, I like that dress. You look great." It really was the truth, but Ted wouldn't let himself think about that. He had to stick to the plan.

A few minutes later, they were out the door and headed for Anton's. They were both painfully quiet during the ten minutes it took to drive to the restaurant. They each had their own thoughts, Chris with her increasingly anxious thoughts, thoughts going from doom and gloom to thoughts of hope and promise, and Ted rehearsing his plan.

When they finally reached Anton's, Ted parked the car and walked around to open the door for Chris. He held out his hand and helped her out of the car. Chris had always liked the way Ted treated her so special when they went out, always opening doors, pulling out chairs, and ordering her favorite wine. His politeness was just one of the reasons she had fallen so hard for him when they first met. They were so young when they were brought together by Chris' roommate, and it hadn't taken long for both of them to fall deeply in love.

They met when Chris was only nineteen and a first-year student at Logan University. It had been her dream to be a nurse since she was a child, and she was studying hard to make that dream come true. Her grades were excellent and her teachers continually reassured her that she had made the right career choice. She had occasionally browsed the stores that sold nurse's uniforms since she was sixteen and even tried on some of the more attractive uniforms. Standing in the dressing room, she would look into the mirror, admiring her image in the crisp white attire, and imagine that she was a helpful, patient nurse everyone trusted and respected. When she had been accepted to Logan, Chris had gone out and purchased her first uniform. It had hung in the closet in her dormitory room just waiting to be worn.

Ted was in his third year at the same university. A handsome young man at twenty-one, he liked having a good time but was less than enthusiastic about his studies. He had made a commitment to his parents, however, that he would graduate and get a degree in Finance. His father was vice-president at H.R. Billingly, a very successful brokerage firm. His father had promised Ted a good position in that firm and a car of his choice after graduation, making finishing school more appealing. So, Ted tried to do his best by juggling his classes and social life. The social activities usually won out, and, unfortunately for Ted, he found himself on probation for the second time in two years. He had until the end of the semester to pull up his grades or he would be forced to leave school.

Audrey Woods, Chris' roommate, was dating Brian Rafferty, a boy who was in the same fraternity as Ted. For weeks now, Audrey had been trying to persuade Chris to get out of the dormitory or library and have some fun. Chris had dated quite a bit in high school, but she was so determined to do well in her nursing program that she had neglected her social life.

One Friday in March, Chris was especially mentally exhausted from classes that week, and she agreed to go with Audrey to a party sponsored by Brian's fraternity. At that party, Ted was so attracted to Chris that he couldn't take his eyes off her. Chris had the same feelings about Ted. He was gorgeous, almost six feet tall with beautiful brown eyes and a lot of brown curly hair. He handled himself with such sureness, and this appealed to Chris.

Audrey and Brian were aware of the attraction between the two; it wasn't hard to miss. When Ted mentioned that he wanted to meet Chris, Audrey helped with the plan to get Chris alone. She told Chris that she wanted to show her the fraternity's library, and once there she left saying she would be right back. A few minutes later, Ted walked with a purpose into the library, strolled across the room to the sofa where Chris was sitting and introduced himself. That was the beginning.

Chapter 5

Ted opened the heavy wooden door to Anton's restaurant. The maître d', who had been there for the last fifteen years, greeted them and showed them to their reserved table in a cozy corner in one of the dining rooms. The chandeliers above were dimly lit, and there was a domed glass-enclosed candle in the middle of each table. The starched white tablecloths shone with an almost eeriness in the candlelight, and the lighting along with the many flowers, plants, and antiques encompassing the restaurant made a picture-perfect place to dine. But they could have been entering a McDonald's as far as Ted or Chris were concerned because neither of them were paying much attention to anything but their own particular thoughts. Ted was the first to break the silence between them after he ordered the wine. He cleared his throat and his first few words came out a little hoarse.

"I'd like to wait until we've had some wine before we talk, if you don't mind," he said, his hands nervously playing with the eloquently folded napkin on his plate.

Determined not to sound alarmed, Chris said, "Is it all so bad Ted, this problem, that we need to get smashed first?" She said this with a smile on her face, and Ted smiled back, his smile just as tense as hers.

"Well, actually, it isn't all that bad, nothing that can't be settled with a bit of cooperating on both our parts."

"You are making all of this sound very mysterious, and frankly you are scaring me, Ted. Why don't you just tell me now? This waiting is driving me crazy."

Fortunately, the waiter came with the wine, and he busied himself pouring it into their glasses. Ted informed the waiter that they wanted to wait awhile before they ordered dinner, thus insuring some privacy for a time.

They drank their first glass of wine in silence, and as Ted was pouring from the bottle again, he looked Chris straight in the eye and told her what a stupid thing he had done. He told her how he had borrowed money from some client accounts at the firm and invested it in their names in the stock market and how he had thoroughly intended to put the money back from the proceeds of these transactions. He told her that his investments, which were supposed to be as good as gold, or so said a very reliable source, plummeted and he needed to quickly put the money back in the accounts where he had extracted them before anyone found out. This had to be done in the next few days, or he could be found out and fired or maybe worse.

Chris sat there, trying to take in all this information. At first she felt relief, because she figured he was going to tell her about another woman and ask for a divorce. But then, after the initial relief was over, she just stared blankly at Ted. Ted's voice droned on and on, and finally she pulled herself out of her unintentional stupor and heard his words. Apparently, Ted justified his actions stating that she and the kids had put such financial pressure on him to buy all the finer things of life, the house, the pool, the cars, etc. etc. etc. Chris listened to all of this until Ted finally finished his speech and looked at him with utter disbelief.

"Wait a minute, Ted. Please don't put this on the children and me. You were the one who was so enthused to buy our big house in Ridgewood. You couldn't wait to have the pool and the expensive landscaping put in. Every year, you were the one who had to have the new cars, the vacations. You insisted on it, if you remember. I always thought this was so foolish, but you were the one Ted, so don't put this on us."

Ted's face was getting red and he almost spat out his words, "Hold on, Chris, hold on."

But Chris was not finished with what she had to say. She was so shocked and mad, just plain mad, that she cut him off in mid-sentence and continued. "Ted, you always told me that you made enough money to do all these things. You showed me on paper so many times just how much you made and what we spent. You always justified all your financial wants to me, and you know I've never been demanding of anything. I have always shopped at sales and even clipped coupons for groceries for God's sake. Don't blame this on me, Ted. I've heard enough." With this Chris started to get up from the table, nearly tipping over her wine glass, and Ted quickly grabbed her arm and pulled her down.

"OK, Chris, let's not play the blame game. We have a real problem here and throwing a tantrum isn't going to help. I've got this whole thing figured out now, so please sit down and listen to me."

Chris felt she had no choice but to sit down and listen. Her heart was pounding so hard, and her whole body was shaking so she couldn't do much but sit down anyway. "All right, Ted, let's hear your plan. I will sit here and listen to your plan, but I will not, do your hear me, will not, take any blame for this. I did not take money from Billingly. I did not take that money and invest it in our names. I did not, did not, did not, so don't you say one word about that, Ted. Do you hear me?"

Ted was astounded by the fierceness of Chris' little speech. He expected her to be shocked, to be confused, to cry, but he didn't expect this. He took a deep breath and prayed that she would go along with his ideas. This was not how he had hoped this would go. Why did she have to pick now to start being so forceful?

"This is how it's got to be. We have a lot of equity in the house, so we can take out a second mortgage. We can sell our stocks, and I can borrow the money from my 401K. This will cover it and I can put the money all back at Billingly. This is the only way, Chris. It's that or get fired or maybe even go to jail."

Chris just sat there taking this in. It took her a while to get her thoughts together, and just as she started to speak, the waiter came to take their order. Ted ordered the special of the day, steak and lobster, and Chris just looked at him in disbelief. "How the hell can you even think of eating at a time like this?" she almost shouted. The waiter took a step backwards and stammered something about coming back in a few minutes.

"What is wrong with you, Ted, that you can even think of eating? This is our life here, our world, all that we have saved in seventeen years. You are sitting here talking of throwing all this away, and you still feel like eating. You are not only a stupid, dishonest bastard, you are heartless. And how much money are we talking about here, you want to mortgage the house, sell stock, the 401K. Good God, Ted, how much money did you take?"

The tears that Ted had counted on at first finally came. But they were tears of anger not fear, and this complicated things for Ted. Instead of insisting or bullying her, he switched his plan to placating.

"Now listen, Chris, please listen. Once this is over, we can start building things up again. I'll still have my job, a darn good job, and there will be promotions, raises. We'll get things back to the way they were in a few years. Come on, Chris, we still have each other, the kids, our health, the important things. As soon as I get this straightened up, we can go back to the way things were with us before. I know I've been a mess the last few months, but it's because of all of this. Chris, please forgive me and help me with this. You know how much I love you and the kids. Do you want me to lose my job? What would we do then? Do you want me to go to jail? My life would be ruined forever. Think of the kids, Chris. How would they feel with their father in prison?" Ted tenderly took Chris' hand and gave it a squeeze. "Come on, baby, help me out here. This was not an easy thing for me to tell you, honey. I did a dumb thing, and now I've got to make it right. Make it right and soon before things get worse. What do you say? Can you forgive me? I love you so much. I never meant to hurt you."

Chris tears of anger became tears of pity and relief. Ted sounded so sorry and so sweet. He had not talked to her so tenderly in months. His behavior these last several months had been about money, she realized. He still loved her; there was no other woman. Just money. And money was never of utmost importance to Chris. She just wanted to be happy, needed to be loved. And when she looked at her husband now, she saw a remorseful, scared man, and her maternal side took over, and she wanted to take Ted into her arms and comfort him. He was her husband, her first real love, and they would figure this out together and continue their lives. They would be a happy family again and things would work out. Then much to Ted's delight, she put her hand over his and told him that she forgave him and that she would help him get out of this mess.

"How much time do you have before things are discovered at the office, Ted? Can we get this together soon? Doesn't a second mortgage take a few weeks?" Chris had a lot of questions that needed answered.

Ted gave her a loving smile. He had won. He was so relieved. He truly felt love for her at that moment. "Well, you see, I've been doing some preliminary work here, Chris. I already applied for the mortgage hoping you would agree. We can go to the bank tomorrow and you can sign the forms. And as for our stocks, all I will need is your signature and we can do that tomorrow. The 401K, that's been taken care of too. So all we really need to do is sign a few papers and it's done."

At that moment the waiter appeared again. He walked up to their table with a little hesitation, hoping that he wasn't interfering in an argument this time. Ted saw him approaching the table and waved him to come over, knowing how he must feel. Ted turned to Chris and asked if she wanted to eat. Chris waved her hands indicating no way, so Ted asked for the check to pay for the wine and they left the restaurant.

Once in the car and as they were heading for home, Ted reassured Chris that things would work out. "We will still have our house. I will still have a job. Nobody will know. Oh! And by the way please don't say anything to anybody about this. I know how close you are to Laura and all, but nobody can know about this, Chris, nobody. I can get in such deep trouble and our lives could be ruined. Promise me, Chris, promise me you won't say anything."

"You know, I'm not stupid, Ted. Of course I won't

say anything to Laura or anybody. You broke the law. You did something illegal. Of course I won't go around advertising that." Anger started creeping into Chris' voice, and Ted started getting nervous again so he took Chris' hand and in his most loving voice said, "I'm sorry, baby, I didn't mean to imply that you were stupid. I'm just so scared and really grateful that you are taking this so well. I was afraid I would lose you, and I couldn't handle that." That should do it, Ted thought. That should settle her down. I just need to keep her settled and happy until she signs all the papers. Tomorrow can't come too soon. I have to keep her happy until tomorrow.

Chapter 6

When they got back to the house, all was dark and quiet. It was 11:00 and the kids had gone to bed. Even the dog was asleep in one of the kid's rooms so she didn't bark and celebrate their arrival. Ted headed for the refrigerator and made himself a sandwich and then to the bar for a much needed stiff drink. Chris' stomach was still so full of butterflies, and the thought of food was not appealing.

She went up to their bedroom and took off her dress. She was surprised that the dress was damp. She apparently had perspired heavily, and when she removed the dress she threw it over a chair—it would have to go to the cleaners tomorrow. She wondered if they would have enough money for everyday things, such as the cleaners, once all this was over, but Ted had assured her that they would be okay, and she had to believe him because she was afraid not to.

She had never been involved much in the family finances. Chris told herself this was a big mistake, and she wouldn't let it happen again. From now on, she was going to be aware of what happened with the money in this family. She had been so scared tonight, so lost, because she knew nothing of what money came in and what went out. How could it have gotten so bad? She had always prided herself on being thrifty and resourceful. She knew Ted made a lot of money. How could things have gotten so out of hand that Ted had to resort to theft? Yes theft, embezzling, ugly words but true words.

The relief that she had felt at the restaurant knowing there was no other woman was replaced by the fear she felt by the loss of security. Yes, she was relieved that Ted still loved her and that she now knew the reason for his distant behavior these past months, but this added dimension produced a great anxiety and unsureness. There was a strong feeling that something wasn't right, something wasn't true. During her quick shower she tried to shake this feeling by telling herself that she was being foolish and that the shock of this all was making her unsure of everything. As she prepared for bed, she said a silent prayer that things would be okay and then went downstairs to look for Ted.

Ted was sitting in front of the TV with a glass in his hand sound asleep. Chris looked at his face, very peaceful now and felt pity for him, along with a strange feeling. A feeling she had not felt before. She wondered about this new feeling, but was too tired to delve into it right now. She did feel differently about him though, disappointed that he could be capable of committing a crime, disappointed that he had used such bad judgment, just disappointed. She took the glass out of his hand and turned off the TV and the lights, glad that she didn't have to talk to him anymore tonight.

She moved up the stairs with a slowness and tiredness of a person who had lived many years. She felt as though if she had one more step to climb she would surely fall and melt into the carpet. At the top of the stairs, she went into the children's bedrooms and took her time looking at them, covering their beautiful, innocent bodies with blankets that had slipped off and surveying their rooms. She loved these children so. She loved her house, she loved her life, she guessed she loved Ted but something was wrong, something had changed, in the last few months—not just tonight's revelation, just something, and she had been too busy wallowing in her own anxiety-laden thoughts to notice.

She crept silently out of Bobby and Scott's shared bedroom and headed for her own bed. Wittles hopped down from Scott's bed and followed her. Chris crawled in between her cool sheets, and the dog jumped on her chest, wanting to play. She grabbed the silly fluffball and held her tightly. Wittles cuddled with her for a while, and eventually they both drifted off to sleep.

Chapter 7

Ted woke up around three in the morning. His body was stiff from lying cramped on the couch. He had a tremendous headache, and when his thoughts slowly began to materialize, great anxiety overcame him, making his head throb even more. He got up from the couch and walked into the kitchen. He needed another drink but knew if he had more liquor he would be even more out of it in the morning. Thinking over last evening, he knew things had gone well. Chris would sign the papers, he would be all right, no one would know, he would still have his job. If it hadn't been so early, he would have called Lisa, just to hear her voice, just to know she was still his. The thought of Lisa made him smile. She was so young, so beautiful. She was exactly what he needed. Now, after tomorrow, she would never have to know how close he came to losing it all.

Chapter 8

Ted met Lisa when she was modeling at the hotel where his company's annual convention was being held eight months ago. She was a tall, long-legged, slender, honey blonde. Her face looked like it was carved out of fine porcelain. Her eyes were the color of a perfect summer sky. Ted couldn't believe that she was in love with him, but she was. The first time they met he had felt such lust for her, and she was a willing recipient of that lust. The attraction was so strong that they hardly made it back to Ted's room before they tore off each other's clothes and didn't leave the room for a whole day.

The convention had been held in New York City, which was almost two hundred miles from the suburb of Ridgewood in New Jersey where Ted lived with his family. For the first couple of months, Lisa and Ted would meet halfway at a motel about twice a week. They couldn't bear to be apart from each other for more than a few days. Ted would leave the office usually around noon and come home very late that night or early the next morning. This procedure got to be somewhat tiresome for both of them and interfered with their jobs. Finally, Ted rented an apartment for Lisa close to him in the nearby town of Langston and convinced her to quit her job, telling Lisa that they could be together all the time when he could get a divorce from Chris.

Lisa didn't mind quitting her job because even though she was young and very beautiful, the modeling business was extremely competitive and she was not very ambitious. She enjoyed her lazy days of doing nothing but making herself pretty for Ted, and lying around the apartment, watching soap operas, and, of course, shopping. Ted was very generous to her. He gave her her own charge cards and never batted an eye when he paid the bills. Some women might have felt kept and uncomfortable with this arrangement, but Lisa was totally content. She knew that soon Ted would be free, and they would be married and she wanted to live in Ted's big, expensive house, once he made Chris and those kids move out.

She had driven by the house several times, in her new red Mercedes convertible that Ted had given her for their three-month anniversary, and she couldn't wait to move into the house and sit by the pool. She could spend her days shopping for expensive things to decorate their house to her own taste. It would be so beautiful when she finished. They would invite her mother for the weekend so her mother could see how well her black-sheep daughter had done. Oh yes, she would enjoy that. Her mother had always told her that beauty was only skin-deep and that she was not beautiful inside, that she was vain and selfish and would never amount to anything if she didn't change her ways. This would show her how wrong she was. Yes, this would show her. She would ask her mother and two sisters over for tea and play lady. She couldn't wait. They would all be so jealous of her house and her handsome, rich husband.

Ted wanted to give Lisa the moon and stars. He knew she liked nice things, expensive things and that was the reason he had taken the chances that he had. At first, it was just the cost of the motel and the costly presents he had given her. Then, there was the apartment and the credit card bills. These bills kept getting larger and larger, but Ted didn't have the courage to tell Lisa the truth. He really couldn't afford all her expenditures. He was afraid she would leave. He knew she loved him, but Lisa was the kind of girl who needed and deserved the very best. He even bought her a new Mercedes when they had a big fight because he hadn't told Chris that he was leaving soon enough to suit her. She was so happy with the car that she stopped insisting that he tell Chris for the last few months.

Finally, in desperation, he started borrowing money from his clients, a little at first, then more and more. He invested most of the money in stocks that he was assured would take off and make a big profit. He was good at shuffling the accounts, paying back one, and borrowing from another. This went on for several months, and at first, most of the stocks did well; then suddenly, they took a dive and he was left holding nothing but a bleak future. He was so scared and angry. He was sure other people had done this and came out of it smelling like a rose. Why did this have to happen to him? He had always been the golden boy. It was so unfair.

Chapter 9

Chris became aware of morning with the sounds of footsteps in the hall, the quiet opening and closing of doors, and the wiggly dog lying next to her telling of her need to be let out. She was also aware that Ted had not come to their bed last night, and this did not surprise her or annoy her. She was thankful. Deep down, she hoped that Ted had left the house and gone to work, but she knew this wouldn't be the case this morning. She remembered the papers that had to be signed today and her heart sank. When she first awoke this morning and her mind slowly began to wake up, she had hoped that last night was a dream, but now fully awake, she knew it was painfully real.

When she looked at the clock, she arose with a start. Only 30 minutes until the bus came to take the kids to day camp. She was relieved to hear that the kids were already up and getting ready. She threw on her robe and fumbled around on the floor with her toes trying to find her slippers. In the bathroom, she looked into the mirror and couldn't believe that it was her reflection looking back. She looked so much older, like she had aged several years. Splashing cold water on her face and brushing her teeth made her feel a little more human. She combed her hair and applied lip moisturizer and then headed for the kitchen.

Becky and Bobby were dressed and eating cereal. Scott was outside with Wittles. Ted was nowhere around.

His car was still parked in the driveway, where he left it last night, so Chris knew he hadn't left. She went into the family room where he apparently had spent the night, only to find a rumpled blanket and a squashed pillow on the sofa. Remnants of a sandwich and pieces of potato chips cluttered the coffee table in front of the sofa along with a half glass of water and an empty Alka-Seltzer packet.

"Good," Chris thought. "I'm glad he isn't feeling good. At least he has the decency to have an upset stomach over this mess." Normally, after having thoughts of unkindness, Chris would hurry an unspoken apology, but not today. Today she meant it.

Wondering where he could be, she headed for his den. As she opened the door, she heard Ted say, "I love you too. See you tonight," and then hung up. Chris stood there looking questioningly at Ted, and Ted looked startled for a second, then quickly grinned and said, "Mother."

"Oh," Chris shrugged. "What's going on with your Mom? She never calls here anymore. Does she call you at the office? I didn't hear the phone ring."

"She didn't call here. I called her. It's been a while since I've talked to her and you know she isn't getting any younger. I'm going to see her tonight." And then trying to change the subject Ted said, "Really, Chris, why don't you call her once in a while?"

"Hey, Ted, don't start with me this morning, this morning of all times. I can't handle a battle with you about your mother now. You know she hates me. Every time I've called her she talks to me for about ten seconds and then asks for you. If you're not home she finds an excuse to hang up as quickly as possible. I don't think she will ever forgive me for marrying her baby boy."

Ted wanted to argue but thought better of it. "You're right. We don't need to get into this again especially this morning. We have an appointment at the bank at 10:30. I know this is hard, but it's got to be done. Please don't look at me like that, Chris. You know I'm so sorry. We talked this all out last night. Let's get this over with and get on with our lives. Okay?"

Chris could not answer. She didn't even want to look at Ted right now. So she turned slowly and went into the kitchen to help the children get ready for day camp. The bus came five minutes later to pick up Becky, Bobby, and Scott, and they ran out the door, laughing and joking, not a care, not an idea of what was going on.

The house was quiet now; the only sounds were the birds chirping by the feeder outside the kitchen window. Suddenly, Chris realized that she was famished. She remembered that she hadn't eaten since noon yesterday, so she poured a bowl of cereal and made toast and coffee before she cleaned up the kitchen and fed the dog. As she headed up the stairs, she could hear Ted in the shower. He was singing. How could he be so happy, she wondered. Thinking it over, she figured that Ted probably had been so stressed over this financial fiasco and was relieved now that it would be over soon. "Well, I guess I can understand that," she thought. "I guess my being mad at him isn't going to do any good. If I don't forgive him it will only push him away and I don't want that."

Once at the top of the stairs, Chris headed for their room. She made the bed and prepared to shower. Ted came out of the bathroom, a towel wrapped around his waist. He looked so young and cute right then and gave her a wink and a smile. Chris relaxed a little then. This was the old Ted; everything was going to be all right. She smiled back and tried to wink. She never had mastered winking without looking like she was being blinded by the sun, and Ted laughed. She walked across the room and gave Ted a hug. Yes, things were going to be all right.

As they dressed, Ted laid out the morning's plans. They would go to the bank and sign the papers for the house, then go to lunch, and then Chris could sign the stock papers when they got home. Ted said that he would go into work after that and make the necessary transactions at Billingly to set everything straight.

At ten after ten, Ted was pacing back and forth in the kitchen waiting for Chris. "Come on, Chris, we have to be there at 10:30. What are you doing?"

"I'm just petting the dog. Give me a minute. She hasn't had any attention all morning. You know how she is." Chris gave Wittles a final scratch, and Wittles followed Chris to the kitchen and sat by the patio door watching them leave without her. Her sad eyes followed every move they made. As the car started down the driveway, Chris glanced at the patio door and never failed to feel guilty when she saw those big black eyes and black nose set in that all white face. It was like looking at a snowball embedded with three lumps of coal. Wittles didn't like to be left alone and didn't care who knew it. Chris, who was always so in tune to everybody's feelings, including her dog, was a bit sad whenever she left her. Laura often joked that if there was such a thing as reincarnation, she wouldn't mind coming back as Chris' dog. Well, Chris had to agree that Wittles was a bit spoiled, but who could help spoiling her. She was so sweet and lovable and so good-natured.

Ted and Chris had brought Wittles home six years ago. It was a week before Easter, and the kids had wanted bunnies that year. They had just moved into the house on Penn St. in Ridgewood about three months before. The idea of having three rabbits in the house, and eventually the garage and yard, didn't appeal to either Ted or Chris. Chris had had a rabbit when she was young, and she didn't think much of it for a pet. She had stated over and over that rabbits were a pain and not much company. She still had a scar on her arm where Bugs had scratched her in an attempt to get away. So, they had put their heads together, bit the bullet, so to speak, and decided to get their then eight-, five-, and three-year-old children a puppy.

An elderly lady, who must have lived in the neighborhood, regularly walked her dog past the house. On numerous occasions, the kids and Chris and Ted had admired the small, gentle, graceful dog, and the lady allowed them to pet him and even let Becky walk him a few times. They remembered that he was called a Bichon, so they went to the newspapers to look and see if any were available. It was Saturday and the paper was small and there were Basset Hounds, Beagles, Boxers, Bloodhounds but no Bichon puppies for sale. They then called two pet stores and were again rejected. The next day, looking through the fat Sunday paper, they saw almost twenty ads for puppies but still no Bichons. Ted said maybe they should get another kind of dog, but by then Chris had her heart set on that particular breed. They continued to check the paper every day, and then the Thursday before Easter, there was an ad in the paper for their puppy. Chris called immediately and made an appointment to see the puppies. They left the kids with a babysitter and drove the forty-five minutes to the breeder's home.

When they got there they were delighted. They were the first people to arrive, so they had the pick of the five beautiful little white fur balls to choose from. The mother was very trusting and let them pick up each of her puppies. After a brief inspection, Chris immediately chose their little girl. She was the runt of the litter, but was the most inquisitive and spunky of the lot. She had just a tiny patch of apricot under her right ear. Other than that she was all white. Chris and Ted were ready to buy her on the spot, but the owners said that the puppies wouldn't be ready to leave their mother until the next week.

After a brief period of panic, Chris and Ted decided that they would, with the breeder's permission, tell the kids about their puppy and bring them to visit on Saturday, the day before Easter. The Collins thought that was a good idea, and so plans were made. When Becky, Bobby, and Scott saw the puppy, they were overjoyed. Scott looked at his new puppy and said in his gentle three-year-old voice, "Look, Mommy, my puppy is so wittle and so wiggly." And that's how Wittles got her name and became the fourth child to enter the Cunningham family.

Chapter 10

The paper signing had to be done at the main branch of their bank, and it took about twenty minutes to get there. Ted was in a great mood, singing along with the radio. He was no Frank Sinatra but he did a pretty good job of "New York, New York." Chris' mood was more somber. She was still feeling very insecure about her life, her home, her family's future. She sat in the passenger's seat, and her fingers nervously twisted the strap of her handbag. She twirled it and then pleated it and then twirled it again.

Ted glanced over at Chris and said, "For God's sake, Chris, stop that, you are making me nervous. I TOLD YOU—everything will be OK. For God's sake." He immediately regretted speaking to her in such a harsh tone as soon as the words came out of his mouth. After all, this was not a done deed.

Ted expected some kind of reaction but Chris just looked at him. She didn't say a word. She couldn't speak right now. She was afraid of what she felt because she felt nothing. No, that wasn't true. She did feel something, but the feeling was better left alone right now.

The car eased onto the main highway where the traffic flow started getting heavier. This was unusual for this time of the day, and it was soon obvious that there was either an accident or construction ahead. The red taillights started to come on, and soon they were driving at a snail's pace and eventually stopped. It was also obvious they weren't going to make their 10:30 appointment, and drops of perspiration started to form on Ted's forehead and face. He started shifting around in his seat and then pulling at his tie and shirt collar. It amazed Chris that she was rather enjoying seeing him squirm. She always made a point of being on time for her appointments, and if for some reason she couldn't make it, it really bothered her, but this was not her appointment and she didn't care if they ever got there. So when Ted started to complain and carry on like a two year old, it was all she could do to keep from smiling. She did keep her smiles to herself, however, and just stared ahead relishing her husband's discomfort in silence.

The reason for the traffic congestion became obvious about fifteen minutes later. There had been an accident where apparently an RV and a delivery van had tragically collided, and emergency vehicles collected on the highway. One lane was open and a policeman was directing cars from one side of the road and then the other. Chris said a silent prayer for the victims of the accident praying that they would all survive and then said a quick prayer for her family, hoping that they would survive too.

All in all, things could have been worse. It was only 10:45, and they were only ten minutes away from the bank when traffic started to flow normally. Ted drove in silence for the rest of the drive and parked the car in the bank's parking lot when they finally arrived. Ted smoothed his suit and straightened his tie when he got out of the car and grabbed his briefcase from the back seat. Chris did not wait for Ted to open the door but quickly got out and headed for the bank. She wanted to get this over with and go home. Just sign the damn papers and get out of the damn bank and go home. Ted quickly caught up with Chris and took her arm. Chris shook his hand off her, suddenly unable to bear his touch.

Ted just shrugged his shoulders and said, "Have it your way."

So into the bank walked these two people, both rather stiff and preoccupied, both with different agendas. They checked in with the secretary, walked into the loan office, signed the papers, smiled at the loan officer, put papers and check in the briefcase, and left. All over. Done. Just like that.

Back in the car, Ted suggested going to the pub for lunch, but Chris said that she wasn't hungry. "Let's just go home and I'll sign the stock things and you can go to lunch on the way to work. I just want to go home, Ted. I'm so tired and don't feel like eating right now."

"I understand, Chris. That's all right. I know this hasn't been easy for you. But, hey, things will be OK, just hang in." Ted was trying to be understanding; after all, he did still have some feeling left for Chris, didn't he? She was still his wife, at least would be for a while until he could figure out how to put all the pieces of his devious puzzle together.

Chapter 11

A knock came from the patio door, and Chris put down her coffee cup and went to let Laura in. She knew it would be Laura. Ted had left about an hour earlier, and she knew her dear friend would be curious about what had happened last night. She had been dreading lying to Laura, but there was no way she could tell her the truth. So she put on her happy-smile face and opened the patio door.

"All right, girl, tell me what's going on. I've been waiting for you to call after Ted left. I couldn't wait any longer. I've been praying for a day now—enough's enough, what is it?" Laura pulled out a kitchen chair and sat down and looked up at Chris waiting for her reply.

"Oh, Laura, it is really nothing. I think Ted is going through a male thing, you know, kind of like menopause for men. He'll be fine, I guess. I just have to give him some time."

"Is that it, is that all, you mean all that you have told me these last several months has been male menopause? Chris, believe me, I'm glad it's nothing really big or anything, but do you believe that, do you believe that's all it is?"

Chris looked at Laura then averted her eyes; she always had been a terrible liar. "Well, that's what I got from it, Laura. I'm not sure that it's one-hundred percent true, but that's all he's telling me now. So let's drop it. I really don't want to talk about it right now."

Laura stood up and walked over to Chris and gave her a hug. "You know, I'm not here to conduct an inquisition. I'm your friend and you mean so much to me. But honestly, Chris, I don't believe you. You must have your reasons for not wanting to talk to me about this and I respect those reasons. So all I'm going to say is if and when you want to talk about this, I will be right next door. If you don't want to or can't, that's okay too. I just want you to be happy, and you don't look very happy right now."

Tears started welling up in Chris' eyes as she looked up at Laura. "Thanks for understanding. What would I do without you?"

"Well, you wouldn't be able to enjoy my chocolate brownies that I just made that are sitting on my kitchen table just waiting for someone to eat them. Come on now, dry your eyes and let's pig out before the kids come home."

So the two friends walked across the lawns to Laura's kitchen. They were so different in appearance but so alike in spirit. Laura was at least five inches taller than Chris, with short black hair and very tan skin. She wasn't what most people would call beautiful, but her caring, humorous personality made her beautiful to Chris and people who knew her well. When Chris moved into the neighborhood seven years ago, she and Laura had immediately become friends. Laura and Don had two children, and the two families had done much together, barbeques, swimming, camping, and short day trips. That was all before Ted changed. For the last several months, he did not have time for his family or his friends. He was always working and away from the house so much. Chris had tried to make excuses for him to Don and everybody else, but Don definitely felt screwed over and the rift was obvious. Don had tried many times to talk to Ted about his behavior but Ted just blew him off. Finally Don just stopped trying.

Chapter 12

Ted called Lisa on his cell phone as soon as he could after he left the house. The phone rang and rang but Lisa didn't answer. Ted figured that she was most likely sleeping or out shopping. He felt a real need to see her, to hold her, to feel her warmth. He was feeling very insecure and frightened right now. For a brief moment, he even wondered if she was worth all of this deception and chicanery. He had laid his whole future on the line for her. He had done things that he would never thought he would do, just for her. And now, she wasn't even home when he needed to talk to her so much. All of the triumph that he felt, only minutes earlier, was fading fast. Of course, he argued with himself, she didn't know any of this was going on today. How could she know that I would need her? To her, it was just another day. He couldn't continue to drive with all of these thoughts going on in his mind. He needed to concentrate on what his next step would be.

Ted pulled the car into an empty parking lot that belonged to some church. He stopped the car and took out his handkerchief and wiped his forehead. It was dripping wet with sweat. He felt all jittery and dizzy. Oh God, he thought, am I having a heart attack? There was no chest pain, no numbness in his arm. It might be a panic attack or an anxiety attack. "Just sit still, breathe, relax, everything is really all right," he assured himself.

He sat in the car for a few minutes, trying to breathe

normally and talk himself out of whatever was going on in his body. There is no way I can go into the office like this. One look at me, and everyone will know I am guilty of something. After a while, Ted decided to quickly drive over to see Lisa. He figured he could have a cold drink and wash his face and calm down. He had a key, of course, and if she was home he could get some much needed loving. He could still get to the office in time to make the necessary transactions and then he would be off the hook and could go back to Lisa's later and celebrate. He really didn't have to worry about what to tell Chris anymore. This made him feel good.

He had only one woman to worry about from now on, just his Lisa. He thought of Lisa with her perfect body, Lisa and her smile, Lisa and their passionate sex. With these thoughts, Ted quickly started the car and drove back on the main road. It was only fifteen minutes to their love nest, and with every minute his anticipation grew. When the car finally turned into the complex, his heart sank when he didn't see the little red Mercedes. She still wasn't home. He looked at his watch and muttered, "Where in the hell are you, Lisa? Damn you, get your ass home." He took out the cellphone again and dialed her number. There was still no answer.

Ted sat in the parking lot for only two minutes when the red car drove swiftly into the complex. Lisa got out of the car, her arms filled with packages.

When she saw Ted her face lit up and her smile was just for him. "Oh, Ted, I'm so glad to see you. I had a great day shopping today. I bought this to-die-for dress with shoes and purse to go with it. Victoria's Secret had a sale and I got tons of thong panties. What are you doing here this time of day? Did we have a date? Did I forget? Oh, Ted, what? You look awful. Are you mad at me? What?"

Ted slowly walked over to Lisa and nuzzled his face in her hair. Just the sight and feel of her calmed him down. "Oh, baby, I'm so glad to see you. I've had a real rough day today and it isn't over yet. I can stay a while, but I have to go back to the office to do some things. Let's go in and you can model those thong things for me. What do you say?"

"Oh, you naughty boy. I know what will happen if I parade around in those panties. You will never get back to work. But, hey, if you insist." Lisa gave Ted her special sexy smile that always drove him quite mad and started for the apartment. She unlocked the door and as soon as the door was closed they were in each other's arms and headed for the bedroom. Both forgot about the thong panties. Their lust for each other was as strong, or stronger, than when they first met, and Ted needed a release from all his tensions of the day. They made love until they were both completely satisfied and then they slept peacefully.

Chapter 13

Ted woke up with a start. The room was dim. He quickly looked at the clock that was sitting on the nightstand, and the digital clock showed that it was almost six-thirty. "Oh shit! Lisa, wake up. Look at the time. Oh my God, how could I let this happen? Lisa, come on, honey, wake up. Oh, shit. Lisa, look, it's almost six-thirty. What am I going to do?" Ted was out of bed in a flash and headed for the bathroom with most of his clothes in his hands. He fumbled with his shirt and pants and then went looking for his shoes and socks.

Lisa rolled over and stared at Ted. "What's the matter, honey? Why are you in such a panic? Did you have a meeting or something? Relax, Tedikins, you can think up some good excuse. It's not like it's the end of the world." Lisa reached up and tried to grab Ted by his pant leg and said, "Come here, baby, let me make it all better."

Ted moved quickly away out of Lisa's reach and almost yelled, "Not now, Lisa, knock it off. This isn't the time. You don't know how I just messed up. Oh, why did I come here? Everything could have been over and done with by now." He grabbed his tie and almost ran out of the room. I'll be by later tonight. Don't go anywhere." Lisa just sat there on the bed with a confused look on her face. Her hair was tumbled and her makeup gone. She heard Ted's parting words and the front door slam. She thought for just a second about getting up, but instead she lay her head down on the yellow silk pillow cover and went back to sleep.

Chapter 14

Ted was really in a sweat at this time. He was hoping he could still get to the office before the night security system went into effect. The last person to leave would activate the system. Once the system was activated, he could still get into the offices, but any transaction after that time was subject to examination by his boss, Larry Moore. Ted drove the distance from the apartment to his office in record time, alternating between praying and swearing. He cursed himself for falling asleep and then prayed for God's help, vowing never to do anything like this ever again. He almost swore that he wouldn't leave Chris, but he knew God would know he was lying, so he didn't go that far.

It was a little after seven when Ted reached the office parking lot. He could tell that his prayers were for naught because there were no cars in the lot; almost everyone left early on Fridays. Hoping for a miracle, he took a chance that someone might still be working or waiting for a ride and went to the door and opened it with his key. When he saw that the alarm was on, his heart sank. He knew he would have to wait until Monday to do all his financial maneuvering. He quickly punched in the numbers and the low beeping stopped, shutting off the alarm system. He walked to his office and sat down on his fawn-colored leather sofa and stared at the wall for a long time. He was completely exhausted. After a while, he pulled himself up and walked to his desk. There sat his computer, looking at him, almost challenging him to turn it on. In a matter of ten minutes, he could have all this mess behind him. But he didn't dare do it now. Larry might decide to check after-hour activities. All this would have to wait until Monday. Ted didn't know if his nerves could handle two more days of worry, but he had no choice.

As he sat there, wondering what he should do next, he noticed a foul smell and realized that it was him. His shirt was very wet with perspiration and was sticking to his back and chest. He removed his suit coat and tie and decided he'd better take a shower. He always kept a spare set of business clothes and some jeans and shirts in his closet. One of the nicer things about working for Billingly was that all the executive offices had their own bathroom, equipped with a shower. He stripped his clothes off and threw them in a pile on the bathroom floor. The hot water felt heavenly, and the pulsating shower head massaged his back and neck until his muscles began to relax and the hard knot in between his shoulders slowly eased. Ted must have been in the shower for twenty minutes or so, and after he finished he quickly dried off and put on jeans and a dark blue T-shirt. He combed his hair and picked up the pile of clothes and threw them in a plastic sack to take home.

By now it was close to eight o'clock and Ted wondered whether he should go to his house or go see Lisa. He decided to call Chris and tell her that he had to work late and go see Lisa.

When the phone rang, Chris hurried to the phone. She had been concerned about Ted. She had worried ever since he left that he would be able to make things right at work and put back the money he had borrowed. It was late and there had been no news from him since they had parted earlier in the day. The children were watching TV in the family room, happy and unconcerned about anything but their own little problems. Chris was glad about that. Why should they be brought into this? The less they knew, the better it would be. She just hoped that they would never find out what their father had done, that he was a thief.

When Ted called and told Chris that he had to work late, she didn't doubt him because the caller ID showed the caller number was indeed Ted's work number. She had been so suspicious lately and did things to check out his stories. A few times she even hit *60 but then he started calling her from his cell phone, and after that she had no way of checking. Tonight, even though she knew he was calling from work, she really didn't care where he was. She was tired and had a sick headache. So when he said he would be late and not to wait up, she was grateful she could go to bed without seeing him. When she asked him how things went at work, he just told her they would have to talk about it in the morning.

Immediately after she hung up the phone, it rang again. She could see that it was Ted's mother and debated whether she would answer it or not. Politeness got the better of her and she picked up the phone.

"Hello, Paulette, how are you doing?" Chris said with feigned interest.

"Oh, hello, Christine. I am doing well, thank you. Is my son there? I need to talk to him."

"Well, no, Paulette, he isn't here right now. He had to work late at the office. I really don't know what time he will be home, but I doubt if he will be able to visit you tonight like he said. Can I take a message or help you with something?" Chris could hear a long deep sigh on the other end of the line.

"Oh no, Christine. I need to talk to Ted about a personal matter and heaven knows I haven't talked to him for so long. He never calls me anymore, and here I sit in my lonely house all day, every day, and feel so deserted. I guess he has other more important things to do than to talk to his own mother, and what are you saying about Ted coming over tonight? Was he going to come over? He never mentioned it to me."

"Paulette, didn't Ted just call you this morning? He said he was talking to you when he was on the phone this morning. Don't you remember?"

Her mother-in-law started to speak, her voice rising higher and higher as she spoke. "Are you insinuating that I don't remember when I talked to my son last? Are you trying to suggest that I am getting senile, young lady? Well, the nerve of you. I haven't talked to Ted in at least four or five weeks, maybe more. And shame on you and the children too. You act like I don't even exist. I've tried to get along with you, Christine. The dear Lord knows that I have tried, but you think you are better than everybody, and I know you have always tried to turn my son against me, and now my grandchildren too. The last time you all visited, the children just sat there not saying a word. They sat like statues. They even looked afraid of me. That is your doing, Christine. Imagine trying to turn your children against an old sick woman like me? You should be ashamed, their own grandmother. Why my friend Dora's grandchildren adore her. They bring her nothing but joy. Just last week she told me…"

The screeching, accusing voice droned on and on, but all Chris heard was that Ted had not called his mother this morning. Suddenly, it hit her like a flash. If the 'I love you, too' was not for his mother, who had he said it to? Chris' headache spiked to a splitting level and she had to sit down. The pain was so excruciating that she felt dizzy. Suddenly, Chris was aware that there was no sound on the other end of the line.

Then after a moment, "Well, well, what do you have to say to that, Christine?" Chris just sat there staring at the receiver and couldn't speak. "Christine, don't you dare hang up on me. What do you have to say? Answer me now, let's get this settled once and for all."

Chris tried desperately to compose herself as she quietly spoke to the complaining woman. "I can't talk right now, Paulette. I'll have Ted call you when he gets home." Then she hung up the phone.

Chris sat down on the couch and put her head in her hands, massaging her forehead and temples. She took several deep breaths and tried to calm her throbbing head. "This can't be happening," she said. "Oh, my God, what is going on, what the hell is going on?" She started shaking and couldn't stop. She didn't want the kids to see her like this, so she quickly ran up the stairs to her bedroom.

Her trembling hands opened the medicine cabinet above the sink in her bathroom, and she knocked over several pill containers before she found what she was looking for. It was a prescription that her doctor had given her several months ago for her anxiety. There were only five pills left, but she almost gulped one down and followed it with two extra-strength aspirins. She had never taken this combination before, but didn't care. Surely, it would only calm her and get rid of the headache. If the pills made her sleep, so be it. Right now, she wished she could just go to sleep and forget everything.

She laid down on their king-size bed in the fetal position and hugged herself with her arms. She lay there for about fifteen minutes reliving the past few days over and over. The 'I love you too' phone call, signing the papers, Ted's unexpected niceness the last two days, his confession of the theft. Things weren't making sense. Or were they? Was there really a theft? Was he making this all up to get money? Who did he say I love you to?

Chris realized that all this speculating was making her head feel worse. She had to try and make herself calm down and stop thinking. She and Laura had taken a meditation class last year, and so she began chanting her mantra. Remembering to breathe deeply, she started chanting "Peace" over and over for what seemed like a long time. Finally, as a result of the medications and the chanting, the headache began to ease and the shaking stopped. She lay there and felt the effects of the tranquilizer and the aspirin. Everything was still the same, but she felt like she was in control now. Enjoying the tranquil feeling, she lay there for a while until she heard Becky's voice as she came up the stairs.

"Hey, Mom, Mom, where are you?" Becky half ran, half walked into Chris' bedroom. "Oh, there you are! Are you sick or something?" Chris lifted her head from the pillow and gave her daughter a smile. "I'm alright, honey, just a headache, but it's better now. What's happening downstairs with you kids? What time is it? Is it time for bed?"

Becky sat down on the bed and looked at Chris with questioning eyes. "Mom, you look terrible. Are you sure you're okay? Your eyes are all puffy. Have you been crying?"

Chris grabbed her hand and held it. "Well, to tell you the truth, yes, I've been crying, but don't worry, like I said I'm better now." Becky scooted closer on the bed and put her arms around her mother.

"Come on, Mom, you can tell me what's wrong. It's not like I'm a child or anything. I see more than what you think I see. It's about Daddy, right? What did he do? What did he do to make you cry? He's been so mean lately, and I cry sometimes too. Sometimes I feel that he doesn't even like me anymore, and Bobby feels the same way. We've talked about it a lot lately. Oh, Mommy, tell me, please tell me what's wrong. Why is Daddy gone so much and such a jerk when he gets home?" Becky's eyes were overflowing as she spoke, and Chris could see the wetness starting to drip from her daughter's eyes.

She pulled Becky to her and held her sobbing oldest child as her own tears started to flow again. She's too young to have to know any of this. This is a time she should be establishing positive attitudes about boys, and how is she going to do this if she feels this way about her own father, feels that he doesn't even like her. Oh my God, if my suspicions are true, what will this do to her, to the boys? Chris held Becky even closer as they cried together. Then somehow she got the strength to pull away. She stroked Becky's long hair, then pulled it back behind her ears and held her face between her hands.

Looking her daughter in the eyes, she smiled through her tears and said, "Come on, kiddo, let's not be so gloomy. Everything will be okay. We are made of strong stuff, us gals, and we need to stop this crying and think good thoughts and all that stuff."

Becky smiled too and said, "Oh come off it, Mom, you're not doing too good right now with all your positive bullshit…oops, sorry." With that they both started laughing and laughed until their stomachs hurt.

Chris then gave Becky a playful push and started to slide out of bed. "Well, come on, enough of this. Let's go downstairs and have some ice cream, with chocolate sauce, and whip cream even. That will perk us all up."

But Becky wasn't going to be distracted so easily. She gently grasped her mother's arm and said, "Seriously, Mom, what's really going on?"

Chris turned and looked at Becky for a long while, and then with a big sigh she shrugged her shoulders. "To be completely honest, I really don't know what is happening with your father, but I promise you that I will let you know the things you should know as soon as I figure it out. All right?"

"What do you mean the things I should know? I'm not a baby like Scott. I'm almost a grown-up, and you need to treat me like one. You can trust me, Mom, you really can."

"I know I can trust you. It's not a question of trust. I just don't know. Come on, let's have that ice cream. I'm really hungry."

Chapter 15

Ted sat on his sofa in his office. He was feeling much calmer after his refreshing shower and change of clothes. For the past half hour he had been devising his plan on how he would return the money on Monday. He figured he would arrive at the office at the usual time, wait until the after-hour security system was turned off, and then tell his secretary not to disturb him. It would take between ten and twenty minutes and then he would be home free and could relax and go on with his day. He would wait about three or four days, or maybe until next weekend, and tell Chris that he needed time away from her and the kids. Tell her that his nerves were so strained by all this financial fiasco that he needed time to himself and that a separation might help, help them both, yes, that was good. He would suggest that she get a job to help financially since they virtually had no money, except his paycheck, now. It would be rough, he knew. She would be furious and tearful. The kids would hate him. But he felt they would come around eventually. He would still have to pay child support after the divorce, and hopefully, not too much alimony if Chris got a job. He would have to get a good lawyer.

His relationship with Lisa would have to continue to be a secret from Chris for as long as he could manage it. Once it was out, the kids could visit with them on weekends or whatever kids were supposed to do, but that wasn't his main concern right now. He liked the kids. They were nice kids, but he had his own life to live. Life was so short.

The big problem now was Lisa. She expected to move into his house and have as much money to spend as always.

The house, mortgaged now with zero equity, would have to be sold. The money situation would change drastically, at least for a couple of years and that would be an immense sore point with Lisa. Their apartment would have to make do for a few years and then with bonuses, raises and such, their lifestyle should be acceptable to her. Ted was very uneasy at the thought of telling Lisa about these financial changes. He knew she liked to spend money and buy expensive things, but he also knew that Lisa loved him. He knew she would be upset for a while, but he would remind her that now they could be together all the time. They would soon be able to live openly as husband and wife, and to sleep together every night. He was sure, well almost sure, he could get her to come around. Anyway, he would just tell her the good news for now and save the details for later.

Chapter 16

Lisa was pacing back and forth between the kitchen and living room. She hadn't heard from Ted since he left in such a panic earlier. Her ever-present fear was that he would just dump her one day for someone new, or even go back to his wife. That fear was very real to Lisa. About three years ago she had been thrown over by Dr. Thomas Riley, a very rich, very handsome internist with whom she had a relationship for over a year. He promised her that he would leave his wife soon, and she hung around waiting while enjoying their luxury hide-a-way apartment, his expensive gifts, and several trips with him to exotic places. They had lots of fun and lots of sex, but one day he just told her that he was going to try and make it work again with his wife. He said his kids were too important to him, and he was feeling so guilty that he was breaking it off. Just like that, goodbye.

He gave her a month to find another apartment or the option of staying on, her paying the rent, of course. She had to laugh at that. On her salary!! So after the month was over, she asked a friend if she could stay with her for a while. Chanray, like Lisa, was also a model and did a lot of fashion shows at various hotels with Lisa. She wasn't really a friend, but they had known each other for a couple of years, and Chanray knew what it was like to have nowhere to go, so she agreed.

Lisa was so furious with Tom, not that she loved him all that much but the fact that he could dump her.

She'd met his wife once, and she was not ugly but she was sure not in the same league as Lisa. It was hard to admit that he preferred his slightly pudgy, unfashionable little wife to her.

All her life Lisa had counted on her looks to get what she wanted. As far back as she could remember, all she had to do was smile and act shy and flirt a little and boys and men were putty in her hands. Even her father, before he left her mother and his three children. Even dear old Dad couldn't resist Lisa. But then one day dear ole daddy just dumped the whole family and took off for parts unknown. To this day, nobody knew where he was. Well, good riddance to you, dear ole dad, who needs you. Lisa's mother had warned her for years that she needed to depend on herself and not always on some boy or man, but Lisa thought her mother was a meddlesome woman who was just jealous of her beauty. In fact, so were her sisters. She would show them someday just who was a winner and who were the losers.

After two months, Chanray told Lisa to get out. She told Lisa that enough was enough; she was sick of picking up after her all the time, tired of Lisa just laying around and never helping, and she gave her two weeks to find other arrangements. Lisa tried to talk Chanray into letting her stay longer but she said "two weeks and out". It was then that Lisa set out to find another man. It wasn't too hard for a girl like Lisa to find a man, but she wanted a wealthy man, one who would provide a place for her to live and shower her with nice things. She met Dwayne at a cocktail party after one of her modeling gigs. Dwayne was a lot older than Lisa, he was rather short and not at all attractive, but he was a nice man, and very rich. Normally Lisa wouldn't have anything to do with men that looked like Dwayne, rich or not, but she was desperate. Dwayne was astonished and flattered that a woman as beautiful as Lisa would give him so much attention. When she suggested that they leave the party and have dinner alone, he was deliriously happy and took her to his favorite French restaurant. They rode to the restaurant in his chauffeur-driven limo where they drank the best wine, ate the most delicious food, and by the end of the evening Lisa was convinced that this was her man.

It didn't take long before Dwayne was putty in her hands. Anything she wanted, he gave her. And in return, anything he wanted, she gave him. Dwayne wasn't married so he asked Lisa to move in with him at his 5th Avenue apartment. Lisa didn't want to seem too eager, so she pretended that she wasn't ready for such a big step. But Dwayne was insistent. He wanted this woman, the most beautiful woman he ever had. He wanted her living in his house, sleeping in his bed, before she got away.

Exactly ten days from the day they met, after presenting Lisa with a diamond watch wrapped in gold paper with a miniature white rose for a bow, Dwayne convinced Lisa to move in with him. Such a coincidence, that was the same day Lisa had to be out of Chanray's apartment.

Well, Dwayne was the one to get dumped that time. They were together for almost a year. During that time while enjoying all that Dwayne had to give, Lisa was constantly on the watch for something better. The day she met Ted, at one of the fashion designer's parties, she knew he was the one. He was tall and so handsome and, of course, she checked him out with some friends who knew that he was a big shot with some financial firm and figured that he must be financially loaded. So it was goodbye Dwayne, and hello Ted. Of course, Ted never knew about Dwayne or her doctor, or any of the others. As far as he knew, she was just a sweet girl from Pennsylvania who made it big modeling in New York, and he was so enthralled with her he couldn't take his eyes off her.

Chapter 17

Lisa almost always attended the parties that took place after the fashion shows where she modeled. There were many, many parties and many, many men. When Ted came along Lisa decided that this was her ticket away from Dwayne. She was tired of pretending that she loved him, she was tired of having sex with him, and she was tired of all the work and late hours of her modeling career. She wanted to watch the soaps, and shop and sleep late and eat what she wanted.

Dwayne had tried to convince Lisa to quit her job and let him take care of her, but Dwayne was always just a life preserver until the right one came along, and she didn't want to be stuck with him with no way out; quitting her job would take away her way out. She felt that a woman as beautiful as herself should enjoy all the finer things in life and not have to be under such pressure to work so hard. She felt she deserved to have some rich, handsome man spoil her, and she was more than worthy of living the rest of her life in luxury.

When she met Ted, she saw all the signs that this was the man that would make that happen. Lisa held on to Dwayne for a couple of months until she was sure. She didn't want to be out on the street again. Dwayne never knew until the end. She managed to sneak away on the days that Ted was in New York. It was easy, actually, because Dwayne was away on business a couple days a week. On the days that he was in town,

Lisa came up with ingenious excuses as to why she was out so late.

So after a couple of months when Ted offered to rent an apartment close by his home so they could see each other more often, Lisa jumped at the offer. Of course, she had to play hard to get with Ted too, telling him what a sacrifice it was for her to give up her lucrative modeling job. When Ted promised she could have and do whatever she wanted, well, she shyly looked at him and said, "Yes, Ted, I'll give everything up for you. I love you that much."

Chapter 18

The ice cream was eaten, the kids were in bed, and Chris was exhausted from trying not to fall apart in front of her children. She felt like her body needed something. She tried to sleep, that was not it. She fixed a sandwich and almost choked with the first bite. She raided the candy jar; chocolate didn't help. She started walking on the treadmill, and she thought she would fall off from the effort; her arms and legs felt like rubber and her chest was so sore from the pounding of her heart.

As a last resort she headed for the liquor cabinet. Surely a good stiff drink would help. Three drinks later, her heart finally stopped hammering, and she felt more relaxed but she was still so confused and mad that she started to cry, feeling sorry for herself. At first it was a soft weeping, the sound of a puppy panting, but then the weeping became louder and louder until she was bawling so violently her whole body was racked with sobs. Wetness ran down her face from her eyes and her nose, but she couldn't have cared less and just sat there until she was cried out.

As she got up from her favorite chair, she stroked the beautiful wine-colored cushions and wondered what to do next. It was three o'clock in the morning, still no Ted. It was very clear now that he wasn't working late at the office, he wasn't playing golf with his friends, he wasn't traveling somewhere. Chris knew where he was. He was with another woman. She wished she had some clue as to who she was and where they were. She would go there and make a big scene. She would storm in wherever they were and say, "You bastard, you cheating, lying, stealing, bastard." They would look at her with fear in their eyes because she would appear so fierce. Ted would say, "It's not what you think." And then he and that witch would huddle in terror. She could see herself grabbing the witch by her hair and…and…and, no, she guessed she really wouldn't.

A weird feeling was buzzing inside Chris' head and her heart. She sat back down in the chair and started to examine what she was feeling. She was feeling, she was feeling that she didn't care. How could that be? She thought about it for a while and asked herself if maybe it was the alcohol, the scotch making her feel so brave and uncaring. Alcohol or not, the only emotion she could identify at this time was sorrow. Sorrow for their once happy marriage, sorrow for the children if they divorced, sorrow for it all. It was such a release, such a liberating feeling. She slowly got up and peacefully walked up the stairs to bed. As she lay calmly, almost asleep, she whispered to herself, "My God, I don't give a damn. I truly don't care where he is or who he is with. I'm just so glad he's not here." As she sank into a peaceful sleep, a smile appeared on her face.

Chapter 19

When Ted finally got to his and Lisa's apartment, it was close to midnight. Lisa was so glad to see him, thankful that her fears of being abandoned weren't real. Ted looked like he had been 'run hard and put away wet' and was so apologetic. When Lisa asked why he had left so quickly earlier in the day, he told her that he had an important meeting, which he missed, and that he was at the office all this time trying to catch up on things. Lisa accepted this brief explanation because she didn't really care about what went on at his office. She just wanted what his job could give her. After several drinks and a roll in the sack, Ted decided he should go home.

It was four o'clock in the morning when Ted got home. He didn't even try to think up a good excuse for Chris. It didn't matter any more. He had what he wanted. She could just deal with it. When he walked up the stairs he looked into their bedroom and Chris was sleeping peacefully. He decided that he didn't want to wake her up and have an argument, so he walked back downstairs with the intent to sleep on the couch in his den. It only took a few minutes before he was sound asleep.

Chapter 20

Saturday morning arrived with the voices of children and the barking of a dog. Chris was amazed that she had slept so late; it was nearly nine o'clock. She felt very refreshed and happy until her recollection of last night slowly crept into the present like a snake coiling around her brain. Then the snake struck and she suddenly felt sick to her stomach thinking about what the day held. She didn't know or care if Ted had come home. She really wished he wasn't home so she could put off the confrontation a little longer.

Not wanting to face anyone yet, Chris took a long, hot shower and got dressed in jeans and a T-shirt and sandals. She then went downstairs to face what lay ahead. By the looks of the kitchen, Chris assumed that her children had fixed their own breakfast. She poured herself a bowl of cereal and put the coffee on to perk. Becky and Scott were watching cartoons in the family room when Bobby came in the patio door with Wittles. Chris smiled when she saw them come in. Bobby's hair was tousled and he was out of breath. Wittles was panting and headed for the water bowl. "Thanks, Bobby, for taking care of Wittles. I didn't realize that I had slept so late."

"Oh, that's OK, Mom, we were just playing catch with the Frisbee. She's been fed, and we fixed our own breakfast. Becky told me you and Dad were mad at each other, and well, we figured we'd let you sleep. Dad is in the den, he's still asleep, at least he was when I looked in the den. We've been trying to be quiet, but you know how that is."

Chris laughed at how serious Bobby was trying to be. She loved her children so much; they were such good kids. "Hey, you kids did a good job, thanks. Don't worry about Daddy and me, I'll handle it."

Just then Ted ambled into the kitchen. Chris looked at him, this man she had loved and trusted for so many years, this cheating man, this lying man, this stealing man. He didn't look so fierce this morning, he looked like her Ted, and she knew this was going to be the worst day of her life.

"Bobby, why don't you take Wittles and go watch TV with your sister and brother, please?" Chris smiled at Bobby and Bobby knew he should get out of that room, fast. He grabbed the dog and was gone.

She poured Ted a cup of coffee and sat down at the table across from him. "We should talk" is all she said. Ted knew at that moment that Chris knew something. Was it about the money? Lisa? He didn't know what she knew, but whatever it was she knew something, and that wasn't good.

Ted tried to smile and said, "What do you want to talk about?" Chris looked him straight in the eye and said, "your girlfriend." Ted felt as if he had been hit by a boulder. He tried to recover by saying, "Whoa, Chris, hold on now, what's this all about?"

Chris held her gaze and repeated, "I want to talk about your girlfriend."

Ted got up from his chair and almost threw it aside. "Enough of this bullshit, Chris, I don't have any girlfriend and you know it."

Chris simply stood her ground and said, "I know, Ted. I know you have a girlfriend, lady-friend, whatever you want to call her. I want to talk about it, now!"

"Look, Chris, you are acting crazy, nuts. I'm not going to talk to you until you stop this. Whatever you think you know, forget it, it isn't so. Do you hear me, stop it!" He then turned quickly around, out of the kitchen and up the stairs.

Chris started to shake; she couldn't help it. She sat there shaking and all her peacefulness went right up in smoke. Maybe she was wrong, was she wrong? Had she read the whole thing wrong? Could it be that Ted was talking to his mother, maybe Paulette did forget. Oh, hell, oh damn, oh hell and damn, what do I do next? She thought of Laura, her dear friend that she had lied to yesterday. She needed to talk to Laura. She had to talk to somebody and Laura was it.

Grabbing her coffee cup, she slipped out the back door and across the lawn to Laura's house. She knocked on the back door, and Don, Laura's husband, opened the door. "Hi, Don, sorry to bother you so early, but I need to talk to Laura. Is she around?"

"Oh hi, Chris, yes, she's here somewhere. I think down the basement. Come on in. I'll find her. Grab a chair and have a doughnut." Don gave Chris a sympathetic smile and left to find Laura. Chris knew that Laura must have said something to him for him to look at her that way, but she didn't care. She liked Don and he was a totally nice man, in every way. Laura was a lucky lady. Don adored her and the kids and even when Chris and Laura were having their 'bitch sessions', Laura could never really find anything too mean to say about her husband.

Chris heard the murmur of words coming from the basement door that was right off the kitchen. She couldn't make out the words but soon heard the sound of footsteps coming up the steps. Don made a quick exit out of the kitchen, not saying a word. Laura went to Chris and put her arms around her. "Hey, good buddy, what brings you here this fine, sunny morning? Good news, I hope." Then, taking a good look at Chris, Laura said, "It's not good news, is it?"

"No, not good news. I don't know what kind of news it is, but definitely not good. I don't know what to do, Laura. I need to talk to you. I need to tell you things. I need your ears to listen and your brain to help me figure this out. I need you to not tell a soul, not even Don, what I'm going to say. You've got to promise me, please, I have to talk to someone, and you're it. OK? Do you promise? Please promise. I can't tell you otherwise."

Laura sat down in the chair next to Chris. "OK, shoot."

For the next several minutes, Chris told Laura everything. She told her about the theft at work, selling the stocks, the second mortgage, the 401K, the 'I love you, too' phone call, talking to Paulette, everything. She told her about her suspicions, and she told her that she was so scared that she couldn't think straight. When she finished her litany, Laura looked stunned.

"That son-of-a-bitch, that bastard. Oh, Chris, you need to get a lawyer and get one fast. If there is another woman, and it sure sounds like it, you need to do something right away. You know, maybe there was no sneaky dealing at work. Maybe he did this just to get all the money. Oh my God, this is terrible. You need some legal advice quick. Darn, it has to be Saturday. You won't be able to talk to anyone until Monday." Laura sat for a moment and jumped up from the chair, "You've got to let me tell Don. He might know someone you could talk to now, today. Think about it, Chris. Time is your enemy right now. You have to do something fast. Don't tell me you want to protect that scum. Think about yourself and the kids. What do you say, can we talk to Don about this?"

Chris stood up and walked to Laura. She put both hands on her shoulders and said, "Laura, you promised. You are the one I wanted to talk to. Just you. Not Don. Not now. I need some time to get to the bottom of this. I thought I'd call Paulette back and make sure she hadn't talked to Ted yesterday morning. I need to talk to Ted again when he calms down and I have my act together. I know you just want to help me, but I needed you to listen, not do anything, just listen. Later, maybe later when I have more information, I will tell Don and ask for his help, but not right now, okay?"

"Chris, you don't understand the enormity of this whole thing. You signed your name on all that stuff. He could leave you and the kids and you'd have nothing. Nothing, not a frigging thing. If you can prove right away that he fooled you, maybe you can do something. That story about the embezzling is probably just another lie. He probably has all that money in a bank account somewhere. You've got to do something now. Please, think about it, think, girl. Your livelihood is at stake here. Don't be so damn nice now. It's time to give him back some of what he's been giving you. Think, some other woman is going to get everything you signed away. Chris, come on, don't be so stupid."

"I know what you mean, but what if he was talking to Paulette, she's an old lady, she could have forgotten. Maybe there is no other woman. What if he did steal at work and my actions get him arrested? What about that, it could be, couldn't it?"

"Come on, Chris, get real, you know Paulette isn't senile. She may be an old bat, but she is still sharp as a tack. You can bet she remembers every day, to the minute, when her baby boy calls her. He's doing something sneaky and wrong here, and you need to get on top of it. You need to stop being so nice and sweet right now and get a handle on what's going on. You need a lawyer and you need one fast."

"Oh, Laura, I guess I know deep down that you are right, and I promise I'll do something, but not right now. Monday morning, yes, Monday morning. If everything isn't crystal clear by then, I will talk to Don and ask for his advice and get a lawyer or whatever I need to do. Don't you understand I need to wait just until Monday, and then I'll feel like it's the right time. This isn't the right time, not yet. I feel it in my gut."

"Good God, woman, you are so dense, but if that's what you want, well, that's the way it has to be. It's your life, but, believe me, if I were you, I wouldn't wait a second longer."

Chris got up from the table, and gave Laura a big hug. "Thanks, kid, thanks for being caring enough to be so honest and even mad at me. The fact that you are right next door helps a lot. I feel better now and think I can handle whatever comes. I'll keep you informed, I promise. No more lying to you." As Chris let go of her friend she noticed the tears in her eyes and hugged her again, this time harder. "Thanks, too, for the tears."

Laura didn't say a word as Chris left her kitchen and headed across the lawn to her own house, but she silently said a quick prayer for her friend who was being so stupid and naïve.

During the rest of the morning, Chris tried to busy herself with routine cleaning chores and conversing with her kids. She didn't venture upstairs, knowing that was where Ted was, doing whatever he was doing. It was very quiet up there, so she figured that he was either sleeping, reading, or watching TV. When he came downstairs around one o'clock, it was a surprise to her that he had two large suitcases in his hands and went directly to the car and put them in the trunk. He returned to the kitchen and merely stated that he thought it was best if he left for a few days and he would keep in touch.

When Chris didn't object, he walked to the car and left. Chris was surprised that she felt nothing but relief. The children, who had walked to the Dairy Hut, were unaware of Ted's leaving, and she planned to say nothing to them when they returned. Their father was never home much anyway, and she didn't feel like making excuses for his actions or explain why he had left.

The day passed peacefully and after a dinner of delivery pizza, and watching a movie on TV, Chris and the children went to bed. The question of "Where's Dad?" never was asked.

Throughout all the years Chris and Ted had been married, he had never been able to really get close to their children. Chris could only explain this to herself by realizing that he had not ever grown up himself. He probably loved them in his own selfish, childish way, but for this she blamed his mother's inability to cut the apron strings, always spoiling him and giving in to all his requests.

Chapter 21

At church on Sunday, Chris tried to pray for her little family, but she was distracted repeatedly by her throbbing head. Alcohol was never Chris' friend, and she had indulged again the night before. She was determined that this would not happen again and definitely not be a nightly ritual. That's all her family needed, an alcoholic mother. Then, after what seemed like forever, the service was over and the kids begged to go to Ruth's Kitchen. It was a ritual they had developed over the years to go to Ruth's for brunch after church. It didn't seem to bother the children that Ted wasn't there, and Chris figured it might help to have some food and strong coffee. The only person who had even asked about Ted was Becky, and when Chris told her he had to go away for business, she just nodded and didn't ask any more questions.

After they had eaten, Chris surprised the kids by telling them that they were going to visit Grandma Paulette. They stared at her with questioning eyes because they knew Grandma Paulette didn't like Chris and just barely tolerated them. But their mother seemed like it was a good thing so they, being children, tried to make the best of it.

Chapter 22

Ted's mother answered the door and the look of dismay on her thin face almost made Chris laugh. After the initial shock, Paulette looked down the sidewalk to the street hoping to see Ted, and when he did not appear she slowly opened the door and invited the four visitors into her house. "Well, well, well, I guess our phone conversation of yesterday did have some impact on you, Christine. Is it really guilt that brings you here, or could I be so lucky that you and the children actually wanted to come and see me? After all, except for yesterday, it has only been five weeks or so since I've seen or heard from any of you. And that includes my son. Where is he by the way?"

"Hello to you too, Paulette. You are looking well." Chris reached over and gave Paulette the mandatory peck on the cheek, and each of the children stiffly did the same. "Hey, kids, why don't you see if you can find Grandma's Uno game? I need to talk to Grandma about something, if you don't mind, Paulette?"

"No, no, I don't mind at all. The Uno cards are in the kitchen drawer just beneath the drawer that has the scotch tape and scissors. Go ahead, children, play with the cards, and help yourself to the lemonade in the refrigerator, but make sure you don't use my good glasses, and don't spill anything and don't touch anything in the drawer except the cards." Paulette motioned for Chris to go into the living room, which was dark and shadowy because the drapes were drawn shut.

The house had an overwhelming smell of roses, the combination of Paulette's talcum powder and the rose potpourri sitting around in various containers. Besides the containers of potpourri, the house was void of any knickknacks and personal objects. The only exceptions were two framed pictures, one of Ted and one of his deceased father. Visits to Paulette's house always felt cold and uncomfortable, just like the owner herself. Paulette motioned for Chris to sit on the overstuffed sofa while she sat in her favorite chair.

"What's this all about, Christine? It's confusing enough that you come here without an invitation and without Ted. So what's the problem? Is Ted sick, is that what it is? Oh my God, what has happened to Ted? Did he get in an accident? Don't just sit there, Christine, tell me."

"Now, Paulette, calm down. Ted is fine. That isn't why I came here. I need to ask you a question, just one little question. Did you or did you not talk to Ted on the phone Saturday morning? Think about it now. You told me yesterday that you didn't. Could you have possibly been mistaken?"

"Is that is the reason you came over here and scared the daylights out of me. Is that the reason? Are you going berserk or something? What is the matter with you, Christine? How on earth could my talking to my own son on the telephone be so important to you to cause all this commotion?"

"Please, Paulette, just answer my question. I'll explain later."

"Christine, look into my eyes, listen to my voice, the

answer is no, no I did not talk to Ted yesterday morning, and as I said previously, I have not talked to Ted, to you, or to your children for at least five weeks. Five weeks, Christine, five weeks. You should all be ashamed. I could be lying here dead and nobody would care. It's hard to be old and alone and have nobody care. If it wasn't for my dear friend Dora, who calls me everyday, by the way, to see if I am well, if it wasn't for her I could very well be lying here dead or injured and who would know, who would know, Christine?"

"You're right, Paulette, we need to keep in touch more. I'm sorry. I'll try to be more aware of your feelings. I didn't know that Ted hasn't been visiting or calling. I just assumed that he was and didn't tell me. But right now I've got to go home. Come on kids, finish your lemonade, put the cards away and kiss Grandma goodbye." Chris gave her mother-in-law a long hug and grabbed her purse and gathered her children and left the dark, cold house with Paulette standing on the porch with her mouth agape and a confused look on her face.

The ride back home was quiet until Becky asked, "What was that all about, Mom?"

Chris just shrugged and said, "I guess we need to see Grandma Paulette more. She is very lonesome and probably scared of getting sick and dying and nobody knowing. She may not be the most pleasant person, but she is family and since your dad doesn't see her much anymore, we need to. We'll all try a little harder, okay?" There had been a long silence and then mumbling of "I guess. If you say so," and "But she's so mean."

Chapter 23

Back at the house, the pleasant sunny day went by routinely. Chris avoided going outside for fear she would see Laura and hoped Laura would not come over and want to talk. Chris eventually curled up on the sofa with a novel she had been trying to read for a week now, but the words on the book's pages were blurred with Chris' own thoughts. Her mind was thinking of how she was going to go about dealing with her crisis tomorrow because she knew she had to do something first thing tomorrow unless she heard from Ted and he made sense out of all this.

Calmly, Chris put the book down and called Ted's cell phone number. The computer voice that answered told her that the cell phone was not on. She decided to try the number later and proceeded to get the kids things ready for their last week of day camp. She packed swimsuits, towels, extra clothes, water bottles; thank goodness they provided lunch so she didn't have to worry about food. After the backpacks were filled and ready, Chris prepared a nutritious dinner of chicken and vegetables with a fruit salad and garlic bread. Her poor children had been eating a lot of junk food lately, which they loved, but made her feel like a terrible mother. Chris didn't know what the future held, but at least tonight, making dinner in her own kitchen as she had done so many times, made things feel a little more normal.

Chapter 24

Lisa was absolutely delighted when Ted walked in carrying his suitcases. "Well, it looks like you finally did it, Tedikins." Lisa walked over to Ted and gave him a big hug and kiss. She sighed a big sigh of relief because she wasn't sure he would ever leave Chris. Ted pushed her away gently and put down his suitcases.

With a forced smile he said, "You'll need to clear out some space in the closet and dresser drawers for my stuff; I'm here for good now." If Lisa could have given herself a 'high five' she would have done it right then and there. But she just smiled knowing that she had him now. He was hers, he and his big house and his money. She would soon be Mrs. Theodore Cunningham. Lisa could almost feel the sun on her back when she would finally lay by that fantastic swimming pool. She could picture entertaining her family and friends and letting them all know that she had made it. Despite what her mother said, she wasn't a loser. She would have it all, just as she felt she deserved.

Ted and Lisa made mad passionate love that night, him trying to release all the fear and guilt he had felt the last few days, and she celebrating her victory.

Chapter 25

Monday morning couldn't have come too soon for Ted. He was up at 6:00 and ready to go by 6:30. He wanted to get to the office by 7:30. He knew that his boss, Larry Moore, always got in by 7. He didn't want to seem too anxious. It had to be just like a regular day. Lisa was sleeping. She never got up until 10:00 or later, so he grabbed his briefcase and decided to hit the local donut shop before going to work. It wasn't until after he had driven several blocks that he thought of Chris and their kids. Amazing, he thought, he was so caught up in his plan to return the money, he couldn't think of much else. He put Chris, Becky, Bobby, and Scott in the back of his mind. They could wait until later.

With two donuts eaten and coffee in hand, Ted arrived at his office as planned, exactly at 7:30. There were two cars already in the parking lot. They belonged to his boss, Larry Moore, and Jed Powers, one of Ted's associates. Ted went in, noticing that the night security system was off. He thought about Friday evening and how he had loathed that security system. Thinking about Friday made him feel cold all over. He tried to shake off the feeling as he walked into the offices, waved to Moore and Powers who were having a meeting in the conference room and went immediately to his office.

Ted opened his briefcase and took out the necessary papers to begin his transactions. He had gone over what he had to do several times so that when the time came, he could do it in the least amount of time. First, he had to lock the door. He couldn't have any interruptions now. He grabbed his telephone and held it between his right ear and his shoulder, so his hands would be free and if anyone looked in his office window or wanted to talk to him he could act like he was on the phone and motion for them to wait.

The Internet was an amazing invention. Money could be moved from bank to bank, account to account in a matter of seconds if you knew the correct codes. It took Ted less than ten minutes to return the money he had stolen and empty his and Chris' accounts at his bank. Well, he was totally broke now, but at least he could relax, he wasn't going to get caught, he wasn't going to lose his job, he wouldn't go to prison.

Ted turned off his computer, got up and unlocked the door. He got a cold cup of water from the water cooler and went into his bathroom. There he splashed water on his face, combed his hair, and straightened his tie. When he went back into his office, Larry Moore was waiting for him.

Ted hadn't known that the quarterly statements were sent out a few days early that month, and as luck would have it Mrs. Levinston had received her statement on Saturday while her son was visiting. When her son opened the large manila envelope, he examined the paperwork as he did every three months. While reviewing the report, he noticed a huge discrepancy and immediately called Larry Moore at his home.

If Ted had managed to return the money on Friday, he could have claimed computer error or some kind of mix-up. But there it was in black and white. Larry went to the office to check Mrs. Levinston's account on Saturday afternoon just after the phone call from Kenneth Levinston. Larry immediately copied the

Levinston file along with most of Ted's other files. He checked all the files against the quarterly statements, and the only file that didn't match up was Mrs. Levinston's. He then checked the current statement against the previous quarterly statement and saw clearly that over $250,000 had been taken out during the last quarter without any authorization from their client. Not wanting to believe that Ted could have done this, he called Mrs. Levinston's home where a distraught mother and son were awaiting an answer. Mrs. Levinston was crying and Kenneth was furious. After talking to Kenneth, Larry was assured that neither he nor his mother had authorized any transactions, and Mrs. Levinston had not received any money in any form.

Over the weekend, a huge inquiry proceeded. All of Ted's files were examined with a fine-tooth comb, and all of his sins were revealed. Someone leaked to the media, most likely the Levinstons, so even if Billingly chose to go easy on Ted, since the money was returned, they had no choice but to file criminal charges.

Chapter 26

Chris had requested that Ted not come back to the house after his arrest and arraignment and he complied. He continued to stay with Lisa. Chris and Ted really didn't talk much. There wasn't much to say. He did apologize for putting her and their children in such dire straits but didn't even try to help by requesting help from his mother. Knowing Ted, she felt he was afraid that his mother would cut him out of her will if he admitted to any wrongdoing, and so he once again put himself above the needs of his wife and children. Becky, Bobby, and Scott were very confused about the whole situation. They couldn't imagine that their father might go to jail.

Then, of course, Ted had to deal with what to tell Lisa. He did not expect her to handle the truth very well, but he had no choice. So when Ted tearfully told Lisa the whole story, he had expected her to be angry but hoped their love would see them through this terrible time. Instead of crying along with Ted, Lisa started throwing things at him and cursing him with words Ted never figured could come out of her beautiful mouth. After her fit of temper was over, she made it very plain to him that their relationship was over and done with. She would never consider being involved with a man who was going to prison, and, most importantly, because of the record he would carry with him the rest of his life, would never have the opportunity to acquire a position good enough to support her in the fashion that she deserved. Lisa told Ted to get his things and get out. Ted did as she requested, with the hope she would change her mind once she settled down.

After Ted left, Lisa screamed, cried, and then faced reality. She couldn't believe this was happening to her. She was so close to what she considered 'making it big' when everything was whisked away. Ted never got the opportunity to see if Lisa changed her mind, because the next day she sold the contents of the apartment to a used furniture dealer, made a call to Chris telling her how much she hated her, packed her clothes and jewelry, and drove to New York in her little red Mercedes, all the while wondering if Dwayne would take her back.

Chapter 27

When Lisa called, Chris wasn't surprised at all. In fact, she was relieved to finally know the identity of the other woman. Lisa was so vulgar and obnoxious that it made Chris feel superior. Chris felt that if this offensive woman was the reason Ted messed up his life, he deserved everything that he got. She only wished that he hadn't taken their children and her down with him.

That was three months ago. Three months of anger, resentment, fear, and confusion for Chris and her children. With every cent they ever had almost completely gone, big decisions had to be made. The house, of course, had to be sold. That was accomplished in record time, because the housing market was booming, and their neighborhood was in a prime area. The profit that resulted from the sale of the house was quickly eaten up by realtor fees and house payments until the house was sold. There were also the utility bills and credit card bills that had to be paid. Ted's company car was returned, and after all was said and done, Chris ended up with only eighteen hundred dollars and her little car.

After Lisa left, Ted moved in with his mother until his trial finally arrived. He was convicted of embezzlement and was given a five-year sentence. Four years of that sentence was forgiven and Ted was sent off to Talbot Prison to serve one year in that white-collar facility, which was nearly one hundred fifty miles away.

Chapter 28

With the date nearing when Chris had to vacate the house, she reluctantly, after every other avenue had been investigated, approached her mother-in-law for financial help.

Paulette was so angry with Chris that she refused to discuss the matter with her. She blamed Chris for Ted's excessive spending and refused to listen to any mention that Ted was involved with another woman.

Of course, Ted had denied that another woman existed. No matter what Chris said, Paulette believed every word her son said. Paulette overcame the shame and embarrassment of her son's actions by telling herself and her friends that Chris and the children were so demanding that Ted felt his only way out was to 'borrow' from his company. When Paulette had asked Ted why he didn't come to her for help, he said he didn't want her to think badly about Chris and the children. Paulette wept. She had raised such a good, thoughtful boy.

Paulette called Chris and told her that as far as she and the children were concerned, she had no daughter-in-law and no grandchildren. She didn't want to hear or see any of them again. The thought of her poor son in a prison just because they demanded so much of him and made him steal to provide all the luxuries that they felt they deserved. They were spoiled, they were ungrateful, they were…blah, blah, blah. Chris hung up the phone.

Chapter 29

Chris spent many hours trying to figure out just what to do. She wished that she had her father to talk to; he would have come up with a solution. But he had died five years ago of a heart attack, and her mother had died two years later. She missed them so much, especially now. Her dad was such a good man, so different in every way from Ted. He was big and tall, had a great sense of humor, and was completely devoted to his wife and daughters. He didn't have a lot of education, but he made a good living working in a factory and provided adequately for his family. They had many friends and their home was always filled with people and laughter. Her mother was a sweet little lady whose job was to take care of her family. She did this very well and seemed to love her husband and daughters more than herself.

Chris had no aunts or uncles; her parents were both only children. Her only living relative was her sister, Marcy. Marcy lived in California somewhere. She hadn't heard from Marcy for two years now. Not even a Christmas card this year. Marcy was what you would have called a hippie in the 60's. She just never grew out of the hippie stage, living in communes and with various men over the years. When Chris and Marcy did get together, for their parents' funerals, they got along great, but Marcy was a free spirit and Chris never knew when she would talk to her or see her again.

With nowhere else to go, and with the help of

Laura's husband, Chris signed up for welfare benefits. She was referred to the Housing Authority where she managed to get a small apartment for herself and her children. She had such hopes that this would be a very brief arrangement, just until she could get a decent job and get on her feet.

Chapter 30

August 28

Moving day arrived too quickly. Ralph Turner and his son, Jack, were at the house at 7:00 in the morning ready to go. Most of the small things had been moved already by Chris, and it took father and son only two hours to load up what was left. Chris had sold a lot of the furniture to a used furniture dealer.

It was such a sad day for Chris and her little family. The kids had all been so upset and occasionally crying the night before. Becky started again as soon as the movers arrived. They didn't want to leave their home, friends, and neighborhood to live in 'the projects', as they called their new residence. Chris had been crying too, but only when she was alone. She had to at least look strong. She continued to tell them that it would only be for a short while.

"Come on, kids, it's only for a few months. Then we can move into a cute little house somewhere near here." Chris grabbed Becky and gave her a big hug. "It will be all right, Becky, I promise. Please don't cry, you'll see. It won't be so bad. We'll come back and visit Laura and you can visit your friends. Please, honey, don't cry." But Becky just cried all the more, and Scott started crying too. Poor little Wittles didn't know what to make of everyone being upset and the furniture moving out the door. She looked from Scott to Becky to Bobby with her head tilted to the side, like she was thinking. Only Bobby put on a brave face, and this made Chris both happy and sad. She hoped he wasn't trying to take on the 'father role' that had been recently vacated. Chris cursed Ted silently and hated him all the more.

When Ralph and Jack were ready to go, they followed Chris' car to the apartment. She asked Laura if the kids could stay with her for a few hours. She didn't want them to see the apartment until it was at least somewhat presentable and didn't want them to stay by themselves in an empty house. So the three unhappy children, along with Wittles, walked over to Laura's where she tried to cheer them up with lemonade and cookies.

Chris was very happy that she had the help of two strong men to move the heavy furniture. Moving boxes, chairs, and bookshelves, along with a few other things the previous few days, had completely worn Chris down. The elevators were working well today at the apartment and the move-in went smoothly. Chris caught a few fleeting glances from the windows above as they moved the furniture into the building. There were several children playing outside who stood and stared, but not saying a word.

Chris smiled and said hello to the children. They were all cute kids who were of different sizes with skin coloring from white to black with all the beautiful hues in between. Some of them continued to stare while two children, obviously siblings, came over and asked if Chris had any kids that were going to move in. She said that she did and gave the names and ages of her children. The children seemed disappointed, because her children were all older than they were. After a while, they all gave up their spying and continued to play.

When Ralph and Jack finished, they left and Chris

started with the unpacking in earnest. It took Chris about thirty minutes before she realized that she had packed much more than the apartment could hold. The kitchen cabinets had room for only the necessities. She put the good dishes and serving pieces back in their boxes, with no idea what she would do with them. The small linen closet in the tiny bathroom could not hold all of her towels or wash clothes, so most of them were also packed back in the boxes. When she went to put the children's clothes in their small closets, she had to pack them in tightly. She didn't even try her closet. She knew there had to be some major decisions on what to keep and what to give away.

After making the beds, and putting the bedrooms and living room in order, it was close to 4:00. Chris still had her cell phone, a luxury she wouldn't give up, and she used it to call Laura. Laura told her that all was well with the children, and she hoped that they would all stay for dinner, an invitation Chris quickly and gratefully accepted.

The kitchen table was piled with five boxes of dishes, towels, etc. that would not fit anywhere in the small apartment. Chris moved them one by one and stacked them in a corner of her bedroom. The bedroom was so small that the presence of the boxes made an immense impact. She knew that she would have to take some kind of action soon to remove the boxes, but she couldn't deal with that right now. Her mother's dishes were in one of those boxes, and some very special items that her parents, children, and Ted had given her. There was no way she would give away most of those things.

She had lost so much the last few months, and she couldn't bear the thought of losing any more. The boxes would stay, she decided. She didn't care if her bedroom looked like a storage unit. The boxes would stay until she found a way to move out of this cramped place into her own home. She swore out loud that this would happen and happen soon.

Chapter 31

Dinner at Laura's house was not a happy meal. The food was delicious, but nobody, including Laura's family had much of an appetite. Little was said during the meal, even though Laura tried to lighten things up with some humorous comments. When dinner was over, the dreaded moment arrived. Goodbyes were said and hugs were given, and there was nothing left except to leave. With a quick stop at her empty house, Chris grabbed Wittles and her food and water dish, and they were off to their new home.

Wittles was very happy to be going for a ride, her favorite thing to do. She jumped from one lap to another and looked out the windows while wagging her tail and barking excitedly when she saw other dogs. After they had driven for a while, the large houses with beautiful trees and green lawns gave way to unkempt city streets and small rundown houses. Glances in the rear view mirror and over her right shoulder showed Chris' three children with wide eyes that changed to wonder and then a bit of fear. Her children had been driven in this part of town before, but they were always going somewhere else, and eventually going back to their home. The realization of their situation was beginning to register and it scared them all. They had heard talk about the 'projects' and none of it was good.

After a brief stop at a grocery store, they arrived at their new home. As they would all learn eventually, a

Saturday in the projects on a nice day was rather chaotic. People of all ages and colors were outside enjoying the warm weather. Young children were running around, while older children just hung out; all were glad to be outside. Some men were working on their cars, while other men and women sat or stood on steps or relaxed on benches talking to their family and neighbors. There was a heated argument going on between two young men that involved some poking in the chest and pushing, but it did not develop any further.

Chris felt lucky that she found a parking place not too far from her building. It seemed like all eyes were on her and her family as they carried the groceries and Wittles into the building. Chris said hello to a woman sitting on the steps that led into the apartment, and the woman responded with a smile. The elevator was working that day and before they knew it they were all inside their fourth floor new home.

The children were all too quiet as they walked around investigating. Chris showed them their rooms, and Becky lay down on her bed and cried. Scott didn't seem to be very upset, and Bobby was holding up well. Chris thought it best to let Becky have her cry while she put away the groceries and put out food and water for Wittles. It was going to be really different taking care of Wittles' needs, no more just letting her in and out the patio door. The thought of going up and down the elevator or stairs early in the morning and late at night was rather frightening to Chris, but that was the way it was now.

Eventually, they all gathered at the kitchen table, and Chris reassured them that everything would be just fine. She would drive them to their new schools on Monday and then find out where the bus picked everyone up.

Chris had been to the area schools where her children would attend and made arrangements for them to start on Monday. The schools were surely not like Ridgewood Heights, but they weren't as bad as she had expected. The principal of the high school where Becky would go seemed like a very intelligent and kind man. He sensed Chris' apprehension and tried to ease her anxiety by talking to her about the school and showing her around. The school was a bit run down and in need of repairs and paint in places, but her main concern was the behavior of the students. She was still touring with Mr. Johnson when the bell rang to signal a change of classes. To her surprise, the students were no more noisy or disruptive at Washington High than what she had seen at Ridgewood High. She told Becky of her experience hoping it would ease her apprehension.

Baker's Elementary school incorporated grades kindergarten through grade eight, so both Bobby and Scott would go to the same school. This made Scott feel better knowing that his brother would be nearby. But Bobby didn't like it at all. He had looked forward to going to Junior High in Ridgewood, and now he felt almost demoted, stuck in elementary school for two more years. When Chris took them to their school on Monday, both Scott and Bobby were surprised at how nice the school was. The school was fairly new, and the walls in the halls were hung with various drawings and projects made by the children. The principal and teachers were friendly and seemed organized. Chris left the school with a happier heart and headed for home.

Chapter 32

When Chris got off the elevator and walked to her apartment she could see a piece of paper taped to her door. She grabbed the paper and unlocked the door. Wittles ran to Chris and bounced around happily, delighted to see someone. She was used to looking out the patio door and watching over the neighborhood when everyone was away. Chris sat down, and Wittles jumped in her lap. The sweet little dog licked Chris' hands and gave her kisses. Chris ruffled her head and patted her belly while she took a look at the note.

Her eyes could not believe what they were reading. She read the letter twice, still confused, and started shaking. This could not be happening. She hugged her dog to her breast and cried in Wittles fur. Panic set in then, and she stood up, still holding Wittles, and walked back and forth for a long while trying to get control. Her head was spinning and her heart was palpitating. She held the dog even tighter. Finally, she put Wittles down, grabbed the paper and dialed the number of the apartment manager given on the note. The phone rang at least 15 times before it was answered by a harried voice on the other end.

"I need to speak to Harriet Gallagher please." Chris said with a trembling voice. When the lady identified herself as Harriet, Chris started to talk, trying not to cry. "Ms. Gallagher, this is Chris Cunningham in Building 6, Apartment 412. You put a note on my door today telling me that animals are not allowed in this apartment building, certainly this cannot be true."

"Yes, Mrs. Cunningham, that was me and if you people would only read your lease you all would know what the rules are here. I was up on your floor this morning and could hear your dog barking away. Now that dog has got to go and go soon, like today. Can you imagine what this place would be like if we would allow dogs and cats? All the noise and stink. It's bad enough around here with all these people, let alone having a bunch of dirty animals."

"But Ms. Gallagher, my dog is so little and completely house trained. She is seven years old and has been with our family all her life. She won't be any problem after she is used to her new home, I promise. You won't even know she is here."

"Yes, I'm sure I won't know she's here because she won't be here. Like I said, get rid of the dog or move out. Do you think you are the only family that needs housing? Why I have a list of people who could move in tomorrow. I'll give you two days and believe me, I'll be checking up on you." With this last remark, she slammed down the phone. Chris just stood there not believing what she had heard.

As Chris looked at Wittles, terror struck her very soul. Throughout the last few months she had been frightened of so many things, but had known she would somehow keep her family together and safe. Wittles was a member of the family too; she and the kids all loved her so. And Wittles loved them all. They were the only family she had ever known.

Chris ran to her closet and fumbled in the small file cabinet for a copy of the lease. She was sure there hadn't been anything in there pertaining to pets. Her hands were shaking as she read over the lease. On the third page, there it was. Only one sentence sandwiched in with some other rules pertaining to unimportant items that Chris had obviously just skimmed over. She berated herself for not being more thorough. She called herself stupid, a dumb ass, a failure. She had failed her family—what could she do to make it right? There had to be some way. They couldn't give Wittles away. It would almost be like giving away one of her kids. They would have to move, but where? How could she possibly find a place in two days anyway? "Laura, I'll call Laura, maybe she or Don can think of something."

It was only 10:30 and she knew Don would not be home, but hopefully Laura would. "Oh, Laura," she pleaded softly, "please be home. I really need to talk to you." Laura picked up the phone after only two rings. When Chris heard her voice she started talking rapidly trying to explain her predicament through her tears. Laura knew immediately who it was. She had heard a lot of crying from Chris the last few months. So she told Chris to take her time and waited for her to speak. "Oh Laura, it's terrible. I made the biggest mistake and now I don't know what to do."

"Is it that bad there, Chris? I'm so sorry. I was hoping that it wouldn't be too bad and you could handle it there for a few months. Calm down now, and tell me about it."

Chris took a deep breath and tried to stop crying. Laura's calm, motherly voice always helped her to be strong. "Oh no, Laura, the place is okay and the kids started school today and that's probably going to work out, but it's Wittles, my poor little puppy. I didn't read the part in the lease that says we can't have pets. And, Laura, the landlady, she's a real bitch. She said I had two days to get rid of Wittles or we are out. What am I going to do, Laura? Wittles is one of our family, one of us. We have to move, that's all there is to it. How am I going to find a place in two days? And we can't afford another move right now, not until I get a job. Please call Don and ask him if there is anything I can do, legally, at least until I get a job and we can move. Oh, Laura, I hate Ted so much right now. How could he do this to us? He's in a nice room in a prison and doesn't have to worry about anything like where he's going to sleep and get his next meal, or where the kids are going to school and what they are doing. And our little dog, my poor little dog, it's not fair."

Laura almost laughed about Ted being in a nice prison cell, but now was not the time to say anything about that. She knew how much Wittles meant to the whole family, and it was so tragic that this should happen now, after so much heartache already.

When Chris finished talking, Laura told her to hang on a minute, she had an idea. She put the phone down and went to her purse for her cell phone. She called Don and after telling him about the situation, suggested that they take Wittles for awhile until things could be straightened out. Don was very cooperative and agreed. He said he felt guilty that he hadn't read the lease himself.

Back on the phone Laura told Chris what she and Don decided. Chris started crying again. "Oh, Laura, you and Don are such good friends. I can't tell you what this means to our family. I will start looking for another place today, and get a job, anywhere, and start saving. But to know that Wittles will be with you, it is such a relief. You are so kind. I know this will be hard for everybody, but it won't be for too long. I know I can get us out of this mess real soon."

Laura and Chris decided that Chris would bring Wittles over the next day. This would give Chris time to talk to the kids and explain everything and give them time to say their goodbyes. Chris just hoped beyond hope that none of them had a bad first day today. It would be just too much to bear.

Chapter 33

Well, everyone got on the right school buses and off at the right stop, and they all three said it hadn't been as bad as they thought it would be. Chris fixed a nice chicken dinner and even made cupcakes for dessert. She took one of her anxiety pills before talking about Wittles. She couldn't be crying now. There would be enough crying from the kids, she was sure of that. So with a calm demeanor she relayed the information as positively as she could. She told them that Wittles was going to stay with Laura and Don and their kids for a little while. She told them that she was going to start looking for another apartment right away, and that all of them were going to be just fine. And she promised.

There was crying, of course, and everyone wanted to hold and pet Wittles at the same time. Wittles knew something was wrong, but enjoyed all the attention anyway. It was a terrible night for everyone and when bedtime came they all had a hard time getting to sleep. So much change had happened in such a short period of time. But they had handled it because they were all together. Now one of the survivors was leaving the next day.

Chapter 34

Morning found the family with no appetite, just tears and long, sad faces. But the three troopers marched off to their bus stops taking with them heavy hearts and red eyes and some hope because their mother had promised. After they left, Chris cried long and hard. Wittles hopped up on her lap and started to lick her face. Chris knew that her crying was upsetting her youngest child so she made herself stop, washed her face and proceeded to take Wittles, all her toys, dishes and food, along with her little bed to the car. It took two trips up and down the dreaded elevator, and then she headed for Laura's house.

Chris noticed as she pulled into Laura's driveway that there were no signs that the new people had moved into her house. The house and yard looked deserted. Of course, it had only been three days. She wanted so much to go in the house and see it one more time. Pretend it was still hers, that her family was still secure and safe, that her dog was still a welcome member. She grabbed Wittles and knocked on Laura's side door.

Laura opened the door promptly and gave Chris a big hug. She then picked up Wittles and hugged her, telling her that she would take good care of her until her Mommy could come and get her. Wittles looked at Laura and then back at Chris and immediately wiggled to get down. She ran to Chris and pawed at her legs to be picked up. One look at her pleading brown eyes and

Chris was crying again. She bent down and grabbed her and held her close.

"Laura, this is so hard, we've had her since she was six weeks old. Please don't let her be scared or lonely. Oh God, how could I let this happen? Everything is such a mess. I've tried so hard to make everything all right for everybody. How could I have made such a mistake?"

Laura didn't know what to say so she just sat quietly and listened. Finally, when Chris stopped talking she got out the coffee cups and poured them each a cup. Chris looked so pathetic sitting there with Wittles. Laura had never had a dog or a cat, even as a child. She and Don had decided that two kids were enough of a challenge, so their pets consisted of a few occasional goldfish, a couple of hamsters now and then, and their bird, Trixie. They had bought Trixie three years ago, and Laura would probably miss her if she ever died, but couldn't image the anguish that Chris was going through.

The two friends talked for about an hour, and Chris calmed down knowing that her dog couldn't be in better hands. Laura had a dentist appointment and so the visit was cut short. After profusely thanking Laura, and telling Wittles that she would be back, Chris left and went directly to the local hospital where she filled out an application stating that she would take any job that was available: nurse's aide, receptionist, maintenance, anything. After the hospital, she went to a couple of restaurants, applying for waitress work. She told a white lie when asked if she had any experience. She said she had worked in Genie's Kitchen for several years serving food, cleaning tables, etc. She didn't mention that Genie was her mother and, in all fairness, she had done all those things, not only when she was home with her parents but also for many years with her own family.

The hospital and the restaurants said they would get

in touch if they needed anyone. Chris didn't get a warm and fuzzy feeling anywhere, but she was determined to continue her search. So she then decided to get the local newspaper and look for apartments and also check the employment section. Chris took the newspaper and headed back to the apartment. She couldn't get herself to think of it as home. It would never be her home because she was going to move out as soon as she could. She knew she had signed a lease, but Mrs. Gallagher had said she would kick them out if they kept the dog. So Chris figured that as soon as she had a job and another apartment, she would bring Wittles back and insist that she was going to keep her, then let the old bag kick them out. Chris laughed at that, and it made her feel better knowing she still had some control.

It wasn't until one o'clock that Chris remembered that she hadn't eaten all day. She had been so busy circling jobs and apartments in the newspaper. She called a few apartments in the area to get an idea of what the rent would be. She was sure to ask if dogs were permitted and hastily scratched out any that said no. There were several jobs in the paper that she felt she could handle and decided to call all of them the next day.

After making a peanut butter and jelly sandwich, Chris decided to go to the grocery store and get a few things before the kids came home. As she drove home from the Pick and Pack, she spotted a liquor store just two blocks from the apartments and decided to go in and buy a cheap bottle of wine. Chris was never a big drinker, but felt a glass or two of wine would help her 'make it through the night'. She had been crying so much lately that her eyes were burning. That had to stop.

Inside the little store, she quickly found an inexpensive Chablis and went to the counter to pay. Behind the small, littered counter sat a middle-aged man almost obscured by the dim light and clutter surrounding him. When he saw Chris, he stood up and smiled with gray teeth and leered rather than looked at her with his small, black eyes. The hair on his head and the hairs almost covering his eyes hung like greasy strips of black yarn. He was medium height, built thick and fleshy, and wore a tan shirt that looked as if it had been worn for several days and most likely slept in. Even worse than his clothes was his smell. It was a dreadful smell, probably a combination of bad breath, body odor, and something else Chris couldn't identify and didn't want to think about.

Chris opened her purse and got out her money, hoping to get out of there as quickly as possible. As she handed the man her money, he grabbed her hand and held on. Chris tried to pull her hand away, but he held on even tighter.

"Hey, little girl, haven't seen you around here before—I'm Terry, and if you play your cards right we could be good friends." He winked and pushed her hand away that still clutched the five-dollar bill. "No need to pay for that, sweetheart, if you know what I mean. I can always collect later."

Chris was dumbstruck for a second; she couldn't believe what he was inferring. After a brief embarrassing pause, Chris found her voice. "Take the money, please. I'm definitely not interested in what you have in mind." She threw rather than handed Terry the money and didn't wait for the change. She grabbed the wine and almost ran out of the store trying not to listen to his raw comments and laughter.

She started to shake uncontrollably when she got to the safety of her car. She quickly locked the door, and only her anger kept her from crying. Chris was mad and humiliated. How could someone like that jerk even think she would be interested in him? Did she look like she was desperate or was he just a foul-smelling man with an inflated ego? She decided it had to be the latter, and after doing a few deep-breathing exercises, she started for home, deciding to definitely never go near that store again.

Once in the apartment, Chris poured herself a glass of wine and waited for the children to come home. Out of habit, she went to check Wittles' water bowl but stopped herself remembering that Wittles was at Laura's house. She reached for the telephone to call Laura and see how things were going, just as Becky came in the door.

Chris put down the phone and she and Becky talked until the boys arrived. It wasn't until after dinner that they decided to call Laura, but her line was busy. So with the thought to call her later, they all settled down and watched TV. A little after 8:00, the phone rang and it was Laura. She didn't sound happy. Apparently, Wittles had started crying as soon as Chris left and continually tried to get out the door. One time she managed to get out when one of her children came in, and she ran straight to her old home. Once there she barked and pawed at the sliding glass door wanting to get in. When Laura went to pick her up, Wittles growled at her, something she had never done before. Laura said that she hoped that things would be better tomorrow and that she would keep in touch.

Chris simply couldn't tell the kids about this. They would not have been able to handle it. She was having a terrible time coping with the situation herself. After everyone was in bed, Chris got out the newspaper again and familiarized herself with the jobs and apartments available. She wrote them all down in her notebook, which one to call first, what questions to ask. This made her feel a bit better, more in control, and gave her hope that she would be able to change their situation soon.

Chapter 35

The next day after the school bus had come, Chris showered and dressed in a navy blue suit with a white blouse with an embroidered collar, put on a pair of navy heels, grabbed her purse, and headed for the first place she had circled in the paper. It was too early to call for apartments and some of the job ads, but there were a few ads for a waitress and for customer service, and one for a receptionist in a doctor's office. She felt it was best to go in person for that one instead of just telephoning.

Chris went from place to place, filling applications, talking to potential employers when they were available. She stopped only for a fast food lunch, and then continued her search until it was time to get home before the kids arrived. Once home, she called some apartments and called about a few ads for jobs. When the thundering herd arrived, she was exhausted but felt invigorated by her attempts to change their impossible situation.

Bobby and Scott were happy to share the events of their day, but Becky was uncharacteristically quiet. Chris didn't delve into her silence, figuring that she was tired or worrying about Wittles.

While they were having dinner the phone rang and it was Laura. Laura was in a panic. Her voice was high pitched and trembling, and Chris could tell she was crying as she told Chris that Wittles was lost. It seemed that Wittles got out of the door again and went to their old home, scratched at the back door barking to be let in. When Laura went to get her, Wittles growled at her and ran off. Laura tried to follow her, but she ran into a patch of woods about two blocks away that bordered the development and was soon out of sight. Laura said she had been looking and calling for her for almost two hours, with no sign of her anywhere.

"Oh, Chris, I am so sorry, I didn't know what else to do but call you. I tried to find her, I really did, but she just disappeared. What should I do?" Laura was sobbing now, and Chris could hardly understand her words. Chris could only say, "Oh my God." She was stunned. In a few seconds, she said, "We'll be right there," and hung up the phone.

Chris told the kids about her conversation with Laura. She told them as simply as possible that Wittles ran away and was most probably hiding in the woods.

"So, let's go, kids, we've got to go and find her." There was a scurry of bodies as they all ran to the car, and Chris could hardly keep the car from flying in her hurry to find her dog. Everyone was on the verge of panic and talking at the same time, while devising plans to find Wittles.

"We should have taken some of her favorite treats," Scott said. "Maybe we can coax her out of the woods with treats."

"She'll come when she sees us, Mom, she just misses us, that's all," Bobby said hopefully.

Becky just sat there, her eyes puddling tears; quiet, deep sobs caused her chest to heave up and down while she struggled to not completely lose it.

Chris couldn't cry, she just drove, determined that they would find Wittles as soon as they got there. Bobby was right, Wittles just needed to hear their voices, and she would run to them right away.

Chapter 36

It was starting to get dark, as they got to Laura's house. The three children jumped out of the car and immediately started to scatter in the direction of the woods. Chris yelled, "Stop!" When they stopped, she motioned them all to come back. "We need to talk to Laura and see where she last saw Wittles. Come here now, let's do this right."

Laura and Don and their children came out and after talking a few minutes, Chris told Scott to stay with Bobby and she and Becky would go together. They borrowed flashlights from Laura and decided it would be best if just Chris and the kids would look for their dog. Chris felt that Wittles might be scared if she saw Laura or any of her family.

The sun was just setting as they ran down the streets to the woods. One of Chris' worst fears was that someday she would lose her little puppy and that Wittles would be lost and cold and scared. That day had come, and she prayed a silent prayer that some big animal hadn't hurt her, or killed her, or that she wasn't lying somewhere hurt and bleeding wondering where her family was. She kept praying as she ran, "Oh, dear God, please help us find her, you know she is one of your creatures, she never did anything to hurt anyone and she was always such a good girl. Please, God, help us find her and I promise I'll take her home and never let her be away from our family again. Just let us find her, OK? Amen."

Once at the edge of the small woods, the foursome broke up into teams of twos. It was necessary to use flashlights now as the sun was completely down. Bobby and Scott and Chris and Becky went into the woods in different places, and started to call Wittles by name. "Come, Wittles, my little girl, my little sweetie," called Becky.

"Hey, Wittles, it's me Scott, come here and I'll give you a treat—please come Wittles, I'll scratch your tummy."

"Wittles, come here, girl, don't be afraid, it's Bobby, we'll play with your bunny ball. Hurry up, it's dark and I'll protect you."

Chris just called Wittles name over and over again as she continued to pray.

After about an hour walking back and forth through the small woods, crunching leaves and fallen acorns, stumbling at times over sticks and branches and trying not to slip in muddy low spots, the disappointed hunting party stopped to plot what their next plan of action would be. Chris was sure that if Wittles had heard them and was able, she would have come to them. "Well, kids, Wittles must have run a little further. Let's try and figure out which way she could have gone."

Bobby asked, "Mom, do you think she just ran off trying to find us? You know you hear about dogs finding their way home all the time. Do you think she is trying to get to the apartment?"

Chris shook her head, "Bobby, this was her home for a long time. She was only at the apartment for a few days. No, she's around here somewhere. She couldn't possibly know how to get to the apartment, and besides she apparently still thinks we should be at our old house or she wouldn't have gone there as soon as she escaped from Laura's house."

Just then Scott came up with an idea. Excitedly he said, "Mom, maybe she is in the yard, maybe she's hiding in the backyard. Maybe after she ran into the woods, she went back to her yard. You see, she got scared in the woods, and she found her way back to the house. She's in the yard hiding in the bushes somewhere. She's afraid to come out because she thinks Laura will grab her. Do you think so, Mom? Can we go and look in our yard?"

Chris looked at Bobby and Becky and then grabbed Scott's hand and said. "Oh my gosh, Scott, that makes so much sense. Come on, let's check this out." They all started running in the direction of their former house. Bobby and Becky got there first and started calling her name. Hearing the commotion, Laura and Don came out and Chris asked them to please go back inside, as she told them Scott's theory.

Chris was hoping and praying that Wittles was in the backyard. If she wasn't, she didn't know what to do next. She couldn't face the thought that something bad had happened to her or that she was wondering around somewhere, lost, cold, hungry, or maybe hurt.

The backyard was very large. There was a swimming pool and pool house, a large patio and a grill area, a huge garden area, and lots of trees and bushes. Chris called the children together and suggested that they all sit on the stone wall that enclosed the patio. "If we sit here and call her name, maybe she will come out, once she knows that it's just us and that Laura and Don are not with us. Scott, you start calling her first. She always comes to you."

So Scott, in his gentlest voice, called for Wittles to come to him. His voice betrayed to all that he was very upset and almost crying, but he kept calling and pleading for Wittles to come to him. In less than two minutes, Chris heard a whining sound. She motioned for Scott to be quiet as she walked toward the sound; her heart beat faster, her hopes rising, the closer she got to the sound. It was coming from some bushes surrounding the pool house.

When she got close, she got down on her knees and said, "Come here, baby, come see Mommy."

A little white furry head peeked out of the bushes, and then ran and jumped into Chris' arms. Chris grabbed her and held her tightly and wept for joy into the trembling dog's fur. The children ran to greet her too, and Wittles wagged her tail and bounced around like a furry ball, licking and barking and just generally being so happy.

After the initial commotion had settled down, Chris had a chance to examine Wittles. She was dirty and full of briars and limped a little with her right front paw. When Bobby shined the flashlight on her, they could see some dried blood mixed in with dirt on the paw. Chris took off her jacket and wrapped Wittles in it and held her close. It took Chris just a second to decide that she was going to take Wittles back with them to the apartment. She was not going to leave her again, although she had no idea how she would manage this without getting kicked out of the apartment. She would figure it out later. Right now she wanted to get all of them back to their apartment and inspect Wittles more closely.

Chris handed Wittles to Bobby and told him to take her to the car while she went into Laura's house and told her that they were taking their dog with them. Laura tried not to look relieved at the news while continually telling Chris how sorry she was for losing her dog. Chris told Laura that she was thankful for her efforts and that it wasn't her fault that Wittles ran off. They hugged and Chris and Becky carried Wittles' bed, food, toys, and dishes to the car. Chris borrowed a carry-on bag from Laura. She figured she could hide Wittles in the bag when they went up the stairs at the apartment.

When they arrived at their apartment, anyone who would have been watching would have thought they were casing the area ready to commit a crime. Hopefully, no one saw the guilty party as they looked back and forth while walking to the building door and up the four flights of steps with their little forbidden bundle hiding in Laura's bag. Once safely inside, the door locked, Wittles was let out of the bag and she started to bark with joy. Chris had to quickly grab her and hold her mouth shut, and they all started laughing with relief and happiness at being together again. They took Wittles' bed and toys and put them in the living room and then set up a place for her water and food dishes in a little corner of the eating area. Becky started to laugh as she pointed to Wittles' possessions.

"Hey, you guys, we went to all the trouble of sneaking Wittles up here, but anyone who saw us would surely have guessed what was in the bag because we didn't, like, hide her bed and stuff. That was kinda stupid, don't you think?" They all laughed again and Chris prayed that no one was watching.

Chapter 37

Chris checked Wittles again and cleaned her little paw. She decided that as soon as everyone settled down she would give her a good bath. But first, she put food and water in the dog dishes. Wittles ate very little, took a quick drink and being totally exhausted, lay down in her little bed and fell fast asleep. The boys went into the living room and turned on the TV, while Chris and Becky cleaned up the partially uneaten supper that still sat on the kitchen table.

As they were doing the dishes, Chris noticed that Becky was unusually quiet. She remembered that she had hardly spoken when she had come home from school and that Chris had been too preoccupied with other issues to ask her what was going on. Now an opportune time had arrived and Chris said, "Well, kiddo, how are things going in your life?"

Becky looked up from her dish-drying and shrugged her shoulders and with a melancholy voice said, "Mom, do you really want to know?"

"What's that supposed to mean, Becky? Of course I want to know honey, tell me."

"Well, Mom, let's put it this way. I hate my new school, the teachers suck, and the kids there don't like me, and they don't want to give me a chance. So I guess you could say that I don't ever want to go back there again. I want to go to my old school. Everybody liked me there and the teachers were nice. I miss my friends, especially Jenny, and I'll never find anyone like her that I can talk to and tell everything to. And I miss Brian, he and I were kinda starting to really like each other and now I'll never see him again, and I'll never have another boyfriend because all the boys already have girlfriends, and I don't like any of them anyway even if they didn't. So, yes, I'm totally miserable and I hate it here and I want to go home, but I know I can't because it's not our home anymore. And all this stuff about Dad being in jail and us being broke is so embarrassing that I couldn't go back anyway. The only good thing about the new school is that nobody knows about Dad and all our problems and to tell you the truth, none of them probably could care less because they all have their own friends, and, like, nobody wants to know about me anyway." Then with a defiant swing of her long hair Becky said, "Does that answer your question, Mother?"

"Wow, Becky, yes I guess that does answer my question pretty clearly. I didn't know you were having problems like that. But really, honey, it's just the first week. Don't you think that if you give it a little time, hang in for a while, people will get to know how nice you are and you'll make friends? You need to be your sweet self and I'm sure things will work out. You've got to give it time."

"Oh, Mom, you are so lame. Didn't you listen to me? Like, all the kids have their little groups where they won't let anyone else join in. Mom, I'm in the tenth grade now, it's not like when I was a child and could go out on the playground and just start playing hop-scotch or other little kid's games. I'm not like Bobby and Scott, where I can join in on the basketball and baseball games during recess. They don't have that stuff in high school, and anyway, I'm not good at ball like they are. At lunch time, it's just, like, we eat and then the girls just kinda walk around outside talking to each other until the bell rings. The boys do the same. And me, I just sit in the cafeteria by myself and try and eat and then I don't know what to do. The last few days I just sat outside by the building hoping someone would talk to me. But now, I've decided not to do that anymore. I'm going to go in the library and read. We're allowed to do that. I decided that I will just read and do my homework during break time. And as far as cheerleading goes, well, I guess that is, like, out. They already had their tryouts and probably won't let anyone else join in. But I don't really care. I don't want to be any part of that school. I can't wait until you get a job and get us the hell out of here."

Chris didn't know what to say. Becky had certainly made her feelings perfectly clear. So she just hugged her and told her that she would try to help her in any way she could and certainly try to move them somewhere else soon. She didn't mention that without a huge miracle, they could never move back in the school system Becky so loved. The price range of the homes in Ridgewood and the surrounding area would probably never be affordable to them again.

"Hey, Mom, I'm going to bed. I'm really tired and I'm sorry if all this upset you, but you did ask."

"Well, yes, you're right. Thanks for being honest. We'll try to work on this together. You just keep hanging in and so will I."

After Becky went to her room, Chris sat down at the kitchen table and let out a huge sigh. This was all getting to be too much. She wanted to ask the boys how they were doing, but was afraid. They both seemed happy. Of course, they were both younger and were good at sports. Becky was right. It was probably easier for them to fit in. Boys their ages weren't as mean as girls Becky's age. If a boy was good at sports, he was probably accepted right away.

So when Bobby and Scott came in for a snack before bedtime, Chris didn't ask them anything. She just couldn't take any more bad news.

Chapter 38

When all had quieted down, the kids asleep, Chris looked through the newspaper again, hoping to find some new ads. Her concentration was interrupted when she felt eyes staring at her. It was Wittles, and she was sitting by Chris' feet staring up with big black eyes, her way of expressing the need to go out.

Chris got up to let Wittles out and then it hit her that she couldn't just open a patio door and let her in and out. She would have to take her down out of the building and find some grass, and it was 10:00 and very dark outside. A little shiver went through Chris at the thought of leaving her apartment at night. She didn't know the area well enough to be comfortable walking outside by herself but could think of no other solution. So she put on her jacket, grabbed a few plastic baggies, and put Wittles in Laura's carry bag hoping that the noisy landlady was watching TV or, better yet, in bed. To help calm her fears, she stuck a small paring knife in her coat pocket. That little knife probably wouldn't do much good in any situation, but it made her feel better knowing it was there.

Chris locked the apartment door and was then faced with the decision of using the elevator or the stairs. Memories of Angie Dickenson, in some long ago movie where she was gruesomely knifed in a lonely elevator quickly resurrected from somewhere in Chris' mind. No, she was definitely not taking the elevator. Walking to the stairwell, she quietly opened the door. As she looked down the stairs, a sour musty smell rose up from the dimly lighted area. Chris thought about walking down four flights of these stairs, swallowed hard, and decided that the elevator was probably the better of two evils.

The elevator door opened quickly after Chris pushed the button. She rapidly scanned the small space and was thankful that no one jumped out at her with knife in hand. After telling herself that she was being ridiculous, she walked in and prayed that the elevator would not stop on any other floor until it reached the first floor. That's how poor Angie got it, she remembered.

Chris sighed with relief when she got out of the rickety elevator. She was thankfully still alive and immediately headed for the door that led outside. She didn't dare go out the front door for fear she would be seen by old lady Gallagher or some other resident that might still be awake.

The door made a loud creaking sound as she pushed open the rusty side door. Surprisingly, the outside was fairly well lit and she went down the steps to look around for a grassy spot.

Chris walked around the corner of the seemingly deserted and quiet building and spotted an area that was part dirt and part gravel. There were a few scraggly pieces of grass and weeds pushing through the ground amid several cigarette butts, food wrappers, and pieces of crinkled newspaper. Chris took Wittles out of the carry bag and put her down, quietly urging her to go quickly. Wittles didn't need much persuasion however and proceeded to sniff the area and then took care of business.

Just as Chris was getting ready to put Wittles back in the bag, Wittles ears shot up and she gave out a low growl. Chris' heart leaped and her hand went automatically into her pocket in search of the knife. With knife in hand, she led Wittles in the direction of the building's door.

Just as she turned the corner that led to the side door, she saw a lady carrying a small dog walking in her direction. The dark-haired woman stopped quickly, looked long at Chris, and started to smile. "Looks like you got you some contraband there, lady."

Chris didn't know how to respond to this woman whom she recognized as the person who lived in the apartment next to hers. The one who had stared at Chris when she was moving in and rudely shut her door without a word.

"Hey, don't look so scared, I'm only funning with you. Look, I got me a little bit of contraband here myself." The lady picked up her dog and pushed it towards Wittles. Wittles started wagging her tail and so did the little brown and white dog.

"See they are friends already. Don't take dogs long to get to know each other. They are more friendly than people."

Chris didn't know what to say, but she did smile back. The woman didn't seem to mind Chris' not talking and continued speaking rapidly.

"I seen you upstairs when you moved in. You know, you and your kids don't look like you people should live here. I seen your nice furniture too when you moved in. How'd you come about to live here at the Willshire Country Club Estates?" The woman gave out a loud laugh at her own joke. "That's what we all call it here. Down on your luck, are ya? Did your old man die or pick up and leave you? Me, well my old man lives with us. Wish he didn't at times. Got a real temper that one. I got three boys, too, sometimes three too many, you know. Anyway, we're stuck here until Frankie, that's my old man, gets a job. Hasn't worked in two years. I work some for a friend of mine on and off in a restaurant and with food stamps and all that, we get by, but I would sure like to get the hell out of here."

Slowly Chris realized that this woman had been drinking and was well on her way to being drunk. Her fast speech and unsteady gait were glaring clues. Despite that, Chris was rather happy to have someone to talk to so she responded by holding out her hand and introducing herself.

"My name is Chris and as you know I live next to you. I've got three kids and yes, I'm divorced, or at least will be pretty soon." And she added, "How on earth do you get by with having a dog here? Mrs. Gallagher read me the riot act when she found out we had a dog."

"Oh, that old bag don't know half of what goes on here. She always checks up on you on the first day, then she is so lazy, she forgets. There is many people here who have dogs and cats. You just have to be smart about it, you know. Hey, I like your sack thing that you hide your dog in. Me, I just stick little Precious here in my jacket. I come down in the morning with her and at night, the rest of the day she has to go in the pan. I put cat litter in there and she goes in there. Didn't like it at first, but she got used to it. Frankie won't take her out anytime. He don't like animals. Come to think of it, he don't like much of anything."

"Anyway, my name is Carla and my old man is Frankie. My biggest son, Victor, is in the same grade as your girl, so he says. Probably my other boys go to the same school as your boys, they never said, but they all look about the same size."

"Well, Carla, that could be. It's been nice talking to you, but I really better get back upstairs. My kids don't know I'm out here and if they were to wake up, they would be worried about where I was."

"Yeah, well ditto nice meeting you too. Hold on a second and I'll walk you up. Safety in numbers, you know."

"What do you mean by that? Is it dangerous to come out here alone at night? I was wondering…."

"Well, girl, you know I haven't had many problems but with a couple of men once in a while and I have got a little scared a couple of times. Like I said, Frankie won't come with me and the boys are in bed, and Frankie is always drunk anyways, so it's just me and my little Precious and she does need some air, you know, so I just come down."

Carla looked cautiously to her right and her left as she opened her purse. "I'll tell you a secret. I keep a knife in here just in case. I put a slit in the side of my purse, right here, see? And I stick the knife in there. When I come down I take it out, just in case, you know. Just to be ready."

Chris laughed and took her little knife out of her pocket and showed it to Carla. Carla laughed and said, "You ain't so dumb."

With Wittles in her bag and Precious under Carla's jacket, the two women went into the building. Chris and Carla both agreed that they felt safer being together and agreed they would try to time their nighttime doggy run for the same time when they could.

When Chris got back in her apartment, she was too tired to give Wittles a bath so she brushed her quickly and they both went to bed. As she lay in bed, she couldn't help but contrast the first time she saw Carla in the hall on the first day she moved in with the sociable Carla of tonight. She figured that the alcohol or pills or whatever Carla had imbibed in had to have a lot to do with Carla's friendliness and directness. However, Chris felt that she rather liked this outspoken woman, and it was a nice feeling to have a potential friend living right next door.

Chapter 39

Chris awoke feeling relaxed and calm. She lay in bed in a dreamlike state until reality slowly swept over her like an incoming fog. She sat up and looked around and realized that they had lived in this place for a whole week. "Well, one week down and how many more to go before we can get out of here," Chris wondered. Actually, if Becky could just find some kind of happiness and the old lady didn't find out about Wittles, it wouldn't be too bad. But Chris couldn't take the chance. She had to get somewhere where everyone could be welcome and happy.

All three kids were still sleeping and she figured she would let them sleep until they woke up on their own. After a quick shower, she put on jeans and a baggy sweatshirt and then tried to get Wittles to go on newspaper because she didn't want to chance an encounter with Mrs. Gallagher. Wittles wouldn't or couldn't go on the paper. She was a well-trained dog and had never gone in the house since she was a puppy. The little dog looked up at Chris with big confused black eyes and didn't do a thing. In desperation, Chris put her in the tote bag and walked down the smelly stairs to just outside of the door. Feeling like a criminal, she put Wittles down while constantly looking around making sure no one witnessed her crime. After a few minutes, she put Wittles back in the tote and hauled her up the four flights of steps. When she opened the door to the fourth floor, there stood an elderly lady who lived across the hall throwing her garbage down the chute. Chris pushed Wittles head back in the tote hoping to hide her, but the older woman just laughed.

"It's OK, lady, we don't tell on each other on this floor. Me, I got a cat, it's easier with a cat than a dog. You just be careful about the man in 3E. He don't like animals and is a mean old man. Most others, they are pretty nice and don't tell the manager lady because she's not nice most of the time."

"Aw, let me see that sweet puppy. It is cute. What's its name?"

Chris relaxed and after a brief conversation, she found out that her neighbor's name was Thelma Weber. Thelma was a sweet looking black lady who looked to be in her 80's. She had gray hair and wore no make-up. Her eyes were bright and kind, and her body was small and plump. She had on a printed, baggy housedress and fuzzy slippers that might have been pink at one time. She had lived in her apartment for almost 15 years and she said that she had a son somewhere in the western part of the country. She hadn't seen or heard from him in almost three years. She and her husband had come to the United States many years ago from Jamaica. He had died three years ago and her only friend except for her cat, a chubby striped tiger named Lady, was a widow named Mabel who lived on the third floor.

Chris liked Mrs. Weber immediately and it was obvious she was lonely. Chris had to almost drag herself away from her neighbor. Finally, after promising to bring the children over later to meet her, she was able to get herself and Wittles back in their apartment.

The weekend went by smoothly. Everyone put forth an effort to try and be cheerful, even Becky. The boys played basketball outside for a while, and later they all went to the grocery store and to Walmart for cat litter and a big pan.

Chapter 40

It had taken Chris a month of applying, phoning, and interviewing until she finally landed a job. She was offered a receptionist position in a doctor's office that was only a ten-minute drive away. The hours were great, no evenings, weekends, or holidays. The salary wasn't so hot, but she figured it was enough to get by for now. She could see the kids off to school before she left for work, and they were only home by themselves for two hours before she came home. Becky had found a girlfriend who lived in the building and seemed happier, the boys had accepted their new life and were content, and Wittles had learned to use the pan during the day; everything seemed to be going well. Chris felt like she could finally exhale.

It had been almost two months now since they left their home. Chris had called Ted's mother when they first moved and left her new telephone number and address, just in case she needed something. There had been no communication from Paulette except she had forwarded a couple of Ted's letters in which he told her how lonesome he was and how much he missed his children and would give anything to see them. Chris gave the letters a shove into the wastebasket. Ted knew where they lived, and he had never once called or written to his children. As for going to see him, that was downright impossible. He was one hundred and fifty miles away and there was no way Chris could drive that far—especially not to see Ted. It was funny, funny weird, that the children seldom talked about Ted, or asked to write or see him. He had been in prison now for five of his twelve-month sentence. Chris wondered just what would happen when he got out.

Chapter 41

Almost every night, Chris and Carla met and went outside together to walk their dogs. It was comforting to both women to have someone to go down the elevator with and walk with in that dark lonely area where the dogs would hopefully not be seen. During those times, Carla and Chris shared some of their lives, good and bad, past and present. It quickly became clear to Chris that Carla was not happily married and that was one of the main reasons she drank so much.

One day Carla confided to Chris that she had an on and off affair with her boss, Vernon. He was the manager of the restaurant where she worked, and she said he was good to her and bought her pretty jewelry and sometimes shoes and clothing. Carla had to hide the jewelry from Frankie and only wore it when she went out. She told him she picked up the shoes and clothing at Goodwill. She said that he was so stupid that he never knew the difference.

Carla said her boss used to take her to nice restaurants and sometimes to clubs where they would dance for a while before going to a nearby motel and have sex. "Frankie never missed me because I would tell him I was working. He was usually drunk every night and passed out by 10:00, and I could have gone to the moon and back, he wouldn't have known."

But now Carla said her boss was cooling down. His

wife was finally pregnant after many years of trying, and he thought they should call it quits. Carla was very unhappy about his decision. She didn't want to give up the good times they had, and most of all she really liked the man.

"I told him that he'd be sorry in a few months when Janet, his wife, was as huge as a watermelon. I told him, 'You'll come running back to me for a good time, just wait.' But he had insisted that it was over because he couldn't chance his wife finding out. He insisted that he was happy about the baby and didn't want to mess things up."

"Things at work are a bit strained, I'll tell ya. For two cents, I'd tell Janet everything except I can't afford to get fired. Not too many places around here where you can walk to work and we don't own a car no more."

On another occasion, Carla told Chris that she could get free wine from some weird guy at the local liquor store. She said that he would let her walk out with a few bottles now and then, and she would give him a big smile and wink. "He's expecting payment," she laughed. "The old coot can wait till pigs fly, and even then I wouldn't let him touch me, but he has his hopes and I do get free booze and wine. Nice set-up, huh?"

Chris was speechless for a few seconds. Surely it couldn't be the same dirty, nasty man she had encountered when she bought the wine.

When she asked Carla, she said, "Yep, that's him—biggest slob I ever met and he thinks he's God's gift, can you imagine?"

"Carla, you can't be serious. That man seems like he could be really dangerous. His eyes are so cold and evil, and maybe he's just a bit off—maybe a lot off. It gives me chills just thinking about him. Are you nuts or something?"

"Oh come on, Chris, don't be such a goody-goody. What can he do to me other than gross me out? Look, I can't afford that stuff and I found a way to get it free. With my damned crazy life I need it just to get through the day. My old man and my boys, Lord, they make me nuts. You got to get over them fancy ideas, girl. You're in the real world now, so wise up and take what you can. You know, I'm no fool, one of these days I'm gonna be old and I won't get shit from nobody. Don't look at me like that, you know what I mean."

"Carla, I'm in no position to give you any advice about what you're doing, you know my life isn't all that great, but be careful with that guy. I've only run into him once and he scared the hell out of me."

"OK, OK, let's let this drop, alright? You lead your life and I'll lead mine. You wanna be my friend, don't lecture me, OK?"

Chris felt like Carla wasn't taking her seriously anyway, so she did let it drop. She was starting to really like this lady and couldn't help but be afraid for her.

About two weeks later, a little after midnight, Carla came to see Chris. She knocked and knocked saying, "Hey, it's me, let me in." Carla was obviously drunk.

Chris opened the door and said, "Carla, what's up? What's going on?"

"Hey, Chris, my dear little friend. Thanks for letting me in. I need somewhere to be for a while because Frankie got pissed at me when I called him a lazy drunk, and he let me have it right on my chin. I'm lucky to still have my teeth. He's such an ass but I clawed him pretty good though. He's got a nice nail pattern on his face. Hey, want a drink? It's a full bottle, well—it was almost full."

Chris stepped aside and Carla stumbled in. Carla almost collapsed on the sofa. Chris didn't know what to say, so she let Carla continue talking.

"Sorry to bother you but thought you might want a drink."

Carla continued chatting away. Chris calculated that fighting with Frankie was a regular thing at their home. Carla told her that when Frankie got drunk, she just had to stay as far away from him as possible, or she would get it good. Carla continued talking about her situation at home for about thirty minutes and then said she felt like it was safe to go back. "He'll be passed out by now."

Chris was thankful the kids slept through the whole incident. She was very sorry that Carla was living like that. It must be hell. No wonder she drank so much.

Chris also thought about the people who lived in this area. Everybody was so concerned with their own lives, just trying to exist. She felt grateful to have Carla and Mrs. Weber as friends. Other than those two ladies, there were only a few friendly faces she would see occasionally in the elevator or coming in or out of the apartments who would exchange a polite nod or wave. They were just all too tired to do more. Chris understood completely. Life was hard and busy, and everyone was dog tired.

Chapter 42

While Chris was busy trying to make ends meet and hold it all together, Ted was serving the last six months of his twelve-month sentence at Talbot, a minimum-security prison. Ted felt, at times, that it was more of a vacation than a prison. He had a fairly comfortable bed, three meals a day, and best of all, no stress. He just did what he was told. Talbot allowed their inmates a lot of freedom. They had outdoor recreational time that allowed them to play basketball and softball. They could also jog and get plenty of sun and fresh air. Inside there was an indoor gym, chapel, library equipped with computers, a television room, a lounge with tables where they could play cards and games with several machines for snacks, soft drinks, coffee and candy. His only job was to help the other inmates when they had problems with the computers.

It wasn't like the prisons he had heard about or saw in the movies or on TV. His cellmates were all men who were incarcerated for crimes similar to his. These men were not violent. They were men who were waiting out the months or years until they could leave and get on with their lives. Most of them had wives and family and money in the bank waiting for them.

That was the big difference. Ted had no wife, no relationship with his kids, and there sure wasn't any money waiting for him when he got out. In fact, he dreaded leaving, facing his mother, kids, Chris, but more than anything he dreaded what he knew would be the almost impossible task of trying to find a decent position with his ruined reputation.

Ted hadn't contacted Chris or his children since he was imprisoned. He meant to, but then time went by and he figured they were better off without him. Scott had Chris mail Ted a couple of drawings he had made enclosed with a short note. Ted meant to respond to Scott's letters, but didn't. After a while, he realized that he didn't really miss any of them.

On visitation day, wives, children, parents, came to visit, but nobody visited Ted. The only time Ted wanted company was when he thought about Lisa and her firm, young body. The days when some of the other men had conjugal visits, he wished he had someone to 'conjugal' with. He had tried to get in touch with Lisa several times but she had disappeared from the New York scene. He did manage to contact one of her co-workers, via computer, but was informed that she had no idea where that 'little witch' had gone and 'good riddance'. Ted figured that she had latched onto the first acceptable and available man she could find—another stupid jerk like himself. As disappointed as he had been with Lisa, it sure would be nice to have her visit occasionally. The thought of their lovemaking always made him horny as hell. She may have been an ungrateful user, but she knew her way around the bedroom.

Ted's only hope of survival when he got out of this place was his mother. He knew she was loaded and since he was her only child, he was hopeful she would loosen up a little with the purse strings. She had written to him almost every week, and he had answered her a few times, explaining to her how little time he had for himself, how awful the place was, and how unfair it was that he was here in the first place. He only did what he did to support Chris and the children. He was only trying to keep his demanding family happy.

His mother believed it all. They did talk on the phone occasionally, but when she cried, as she always did, he made excuses to quickly get off the phone. She was lonely and she was not well; he had heard it so many times. She told him over and over that no matter how lonely she was she would not call her ex-daughter-in-law or her grandchildren because they were the ungrateful people responsible for her son's misery and fall from grace.

Chapter 43

Lisa had driven back to New York in her red Mercedes as fast as she could after Ted told her he was going to prison. The first thing she had to do was find Dwayne, the man who was her lover before she moved to New Jersey to be with Ted. Their parting had not been pleasant. She told Dwayne that he was an ugly little man and a lousy lover. She had laughed in his face and left him red-faced with anger. She figured this wasn't going to be an easy sell, but she wasn't about to go back to the grueling work of modeling. She felt that she was too good to work after all the months of living like a princess.

Ted had been such a disappointment. She really thought she had found the perfect man. Good looks, money, hot sex, crazy about her, everything Lisa wanted in a man. Thinking about Ted, she sometimes missed him, or was it the prospect of living in his big house and lounging by that impressive in-ground pool that she really missed. That and her expectations of lording her new life over her family and friends. She hadn't talked to her family about her split from Ted. She knew exactly what her mother would say and didn't want to hear it.

When she got back to New York, Lisa got an inexpensive hotel for a few days until she could figure out her next move. She was in a tough spot as far as money was concerned. She had some cash from the sale of the apartment furniture, but Ted had canceled all her credit cards and her account at the bank. She most surely wasn't going to sell her car; how many times in a girl's life does someone give you a Mercedes!

Her first move was to get in contact with some of her old friends. She wasn't going to tell them the truth, of course; she would tell them that she was bored with Ted and needed some excitement, so she left him. Some of the girls wouldn't believe her, but she would stick to her story and not give a care what anybody thought.

She casually asked around about Dwayne. Belinda Knowles was happy to tell her all the latest gossip surrounding Dwayne. Lisa was absolutely shocked to hear that he was recently married to Dianna Wilson, a very successful agent to some high-powered models. Dwayne and Dianna had married only three weeks ago and were now traveling around the world on their honeymoon. Lisa was furious. It could have been her. She blamed Ted and cussed him under her breath while she smiled at the good news, not wanting Belinda to know how she felt. Belinda then told her how miserable Dwayne had been after she left him and how he had gone into a slight depression. His depressed state didn't last long when news got out that such a wealthy man was back in circulation. Despite his uninteresting looks and personality, the vultures circled and Dianna caught the prey. Dianna was getting tired of her hectic life and needed an out. Dwayne was it. After dating for a while, the two seemed to have formed a fondness for each other and Dwayne proposed. From then on, Dianna's life was like royalty. She had the luxury of traveling in his white stretch limo, ate at the most popular restaurants, bought only designer clothes, and partied with the best people. Her diamond engagement ring was so big and beautiful; it was featured in the bridal section of the *New York Times*.

Belinda enthusiastically went on and on, going into quite a bit of detail, especially about Dianna and

Dwayne's wedding day. She described the gown and veil, the flowers, the food served, the famous band that played during the reception, every little detail. Lisa was screaming inside her head. All of that could have been hers. How had she let it get away, especially for a crook and loser like Ted?

She had had Dwayne in the palm of her hand. She could now be traveling around the world. She could be living the life she so deserved. How had she been so stupid? Suddenly, all Dwayne's undesirable qualities didn't seem so undesirable. In her mind's eye Dwayne had grown a few inches taller, his face more handsome, his personality less boring. What had she done?

As Belinda droned on and on, Lisa felt a real need to get away from her, fast. She could not bear to hear any more details about Dianna's wonderful life. She was feeling physically sick. So pretending to have an important engagement, Lisa quickly left Belinda and hurried back to her hotel to think things over and plan her next move.

Back in her room, Lisa's mind was reeling. She went over and over all that happened in the last several months. If she could have kicked herself, she would have. Instead, she did something that she hadn't done in years. She cried. She sobbed. She screamed into her pillow so that nobody could hear her. This went on for over an hour until her eyes were puffy and sore and she had a splitting headache. When she went to find some aspirin in her medicine kit, she glanced into the bathroom mirror. Lisa couldn't believe how terrible she looked. The shock of her red eyes and swollen face propelled her back to reality.

She couldn't let this situation ruin her life, her good looks. Now, more than ever, she would have to depend on her beautiful face and figure. After washing her face with her expensive moisturizing soap, and splashing over and over with cold water, she applied her night cream, put on her nightgown and went to bed. She would figure out her next step tomorrow after a good night's sleep.

Hours later, her sheets and blanket all tangled and rumpled, Lisa finally gave up on sleep. She went directly to the mini-bar across from her bed and took out three little bottles. She threw on her robe, grabbed the empty ice bucket, and set out to find the ice machine.

She assumed it was early morning because the halls were empty and very quiet. As Lisa walked around the hall, looking for the cubbyhole that held the ice and snack machines, she passed the elevator. As luck would have it she heard a ding, and the doors opened. The last thing she wanted was to see another human being right now. However, not only did one person exit the elevator, but a line of noisy, obviously drunk men tumbled out talking and laughing loudly. Lisa hung her head down and walked fast trying to be invisible.

When the crew of inebriated men saw her, there were catcalls and some rowdy comments. Lisa walked faster—all she wanted now was to get back to her room. All but two of the men headed to their rooms, going in the opposite direction from where Lisa was quickly walking. The other two men obviously were not finished partying and had hopes of finding a playmate for the night. They followed Lisa closely, suggesting that she join them in various activities. Money was offered. Lisa continued to walk fast, now almost at a run. When she realized that the men were right behind her, she turned and told them that if they didn't leave her alone she would scream as loudly as she could and hopefully wake up the entire population of the sixth floor.

One of the men, obviously just out for a good time,

and not wanting any trouble or notoriety, held out his hands as in surrender. He said that they would gladly back off and surely she couldn't fault them for trying. Lisa didn't stick around long enough to answer. She forgot about the ice and raced to her room.

Back in the safety of her room, she drank the little bottles without ice. She was shaking so badly that she spilled one of them down the front of her robe. Then she started to cry again. She damned all men to hell and wept so hard that she got the hiccups. How could all this be happening to her? First losing Ted because he was a crook and a liar. Then finding out that she could have been living in luxury if she had only held onto that creep Dwayne. Now what was there to look forward to—just more work with the modeling agencies: hard work, long hours under hot lights that dried up her skin. Early mornings, lord how she hated early mornings and all that smiling when she didn't feel like smiling. Being nice to all those horrible people, those lecherous men who just wanted to leer at her and get her into bed. Not too long ago she could have handled all this, even thought some of it was fun. Now, she really just wanted someone, someone rich, to take care of her.

Lisa got two more little bottles out of the mini-bar and rapidly consumed them. Between the sobbing and the booze, in addition to now being 5:30 in then morning, exhaustion finally took over and Lisa fell asleep. She dreamed fitfully for several hours and her dreams were mean, the kind of dreams where you would like to wake up and almost do, but get pulled back in time after time.

Lisa slept until early afternoon. When she finally awoke, she felt like she had been 'rode hard and put away wet'. A glance in the mirror made her start. Red eyes with crinkles around them looked back at her. Her skin was dry from too much alcohol, and she felt like she had gained five pounds. She sure couldn't get her job back looking like an old lady. So she decided to stay in the room for however long it took to repair the damage.

For two days she did not leave; she ordered salads and bottled water from room service and took long baths and piled on the moisturizers. She exercised with some guy on TV and did extra sit-ups. She was thankful that she was still young enough for her skin to bounce back as quickly as it did. After only two days, she felt that she was ready to face the world again.

Chapter 44

Lisa had been gone from New York for over six months, but her old agent's office looked exactly the same. Lisa was glad that she had always had a good rapport with Miranda, her agent. When she quit and went away with Ted, they had parted amiably.

Lisa walked into Miranda's outer office. The elegant waiting room was empty, and Fran, Miranda's long-time secretary, was not at her desk. Miranda's door was open a few inches and Lisa could hear her talking on the phone.

Lisa knew it was Miranda by her low, raspy, three-packs-a-day voice, accompanied by a deep cough, that got worse with each passing year. She waited until the telephone call ended and peeked around the door and with a smile said, "She's back." Miranda got up and gave Lisa a big hug and invited her into her office. She was truly glad to see Lisa; they always had a good working relationship as well as a fondness for each other. Lisa explained that her relationship with Ted had not worked out, and of course, she omitted the parts about stealing and prison. Miranda listened with sincere sympathy as Lisa explained her urgent need to start working again. Miranda was genuinely understanding of Lisa's situation. She had been on her own most of her life and knew how hard life could be when you had only yourself to survive in this man's world.

After talking for a long while, Miranda assured Lisa that she would be delighted to represent her again. She had always been able to place Lisa quickly in good paying shoots. Lisa had the look that most clients found irresistible.

Chapter 45

Chris woke up to a pounding noise. Someone was knocking on her door. She looked at the alarm clock and it said 3:15. Her heart jumped. "Who could be at the door at this time of night?" She quickly checked the children and the noise hadn't awakened them. Wittles started to growl but she quieted her before she could start to bark.

Grabbing her robe, she headed for the door. There was no peephole on the door so she couldn't see out. As she was deciding what to do, she heard Carla's voice. "Come on, Chris, open up. I need you."

Chris opened the door and was shocked by what she saw. There stood Carla, blood running down her face. Her right eye was swollen almost twice its size and she was sobbing. Her blouse was torn by her shoulder, and it was spotted with blood that came from somewhere on her face; it was hard to tell where. Carla stumbled and almost fell into the room.

"Oh my God, Carla, what happened to you? Are you all right? Should I call an ambulance? What happened?"

"No, no, don't call no ambulance. I'll be OK in a minute. I just needed to get away from Frankie before he can get at me again."

"Frankie did this to you? Oh, Carla, how could he do this? Here, sit down here while I get a washcloth and some ice."

"Thanks, kid, I'm sorry to come over like this, but I just didn't know what to do and I don't have no place else to go."

Chris told Carla to try and be still and calm down as she tried to gently wash the blood from her face. As she removed the blood with the cloth, she found that most of the blood stemmed from Carla's left ear where it was torn and oozing. She held the compress on the wound for a while until the blood slowed and then put on a butterfly bandage. Chris then got some ice from the freezer for Carla's swollen eye and led Carla to the couch where she helped her lay down. It wasn't until then that Carla began talking about what had occurred that evening.

"Of all nights for him to be awake. I guess he had the trots or something and wasn't able to sleep. When I walked in the door and he saw what time it was and took a look at my torn blouse, he just got mean with me and started accusing me of all kind of crap. He started hollerin' and calling me a whore. He wanted to know who I had been with and wanted to know his name. He said he was gonna kick his ass."

"I told him to shut up and take his drunken butt to bed. He laughed and said he hoped that I was better in bed with my lover than I was with him. He was so loud that he woke up the boys. Victor got in Frankie's face and told him to leave me alone. Frankie started cussin' out Victor and started toward him. Frankie was wobbling, he was so damn drunk, and when he lunged at Victor he fell down right on his ass. I got in between them and told Victor to go bed and I would handle things. Just then Frankie caught me off guard, grabbed my leg and pulled me down and started punching me. Then all three boys held Frankie down while I got away from him. I grabbed the phone and told Frankie that I was going to call the police if he didn't stop acting like a damn fool."

"Well, he knew I meant it and got up and headed for the bed mumbling that I was, well, I won't tell you all he said. He said some pretty rotten stuff. I got the boys calmed down and back to bed, but I just couldn't even think about sleeping. I was so mad at myself. I can usually get away from him when he gets like that, but I guess I did let my guard down for a second."

"Carla, I know you told me Frankie can be violent but this is terrible. How can you live like this knowing he could hurt you at anytime?"

"What choice do I have, Chris? When that bum gets loaded, he turns into a real Dr. Jekyll, or is Mr. Hyde the bad one? I learned to just let him alone or leave. He won't hurt the boys; he never has. I'm his punching bag when he can get at me. Oh, ouch, my ear and my eye are killing me. Do you have any pills or booze?"

Chris could detect a strong smell of liquor on Carla and decided that giving her more would not be wise. So she got some aspirin from the bathroom cabinet and gave her two.

"Is this it? Is this all you have? I could use a good stiff drink right now, Chris."

"Well, to tell you the truth, I don't have anything stronger than Pepsi in the house at the moment. So these will have to do."

Carla looked disappointed but didn't say anything. She was just happy to have Chris' help and a place to rest until Frankie fell asleep.

"Uh, Carla, not to be intrusive but you said you came in late and your blouse was torn. Do you want to talk about that? If not, please don't. I was just wondering."

Carla paused for a long time and then told Chris that she had been working that night, and during her break she almost begged Vernon to talk to her about his decision to break things off with her.

"After the restaurant closed we sat in one of the booths and I told him that I really did love him and couldn't handle his decision to end the good thing we have going. You know, Chris, we have been lovers for almost four years now. I'm sure not proud of the fact that I made a complete ass of myself. I was really pleading with him and I cried, and I haven't cried in years. At first he just repeated that he was going to try and make it with his wife because she was pregnant and due to deliver in a couple of months. They hadn't been able to have kids before now. He told me again that it had to be over and that if I couldn't accept it he would have to fire me. When I kept at him he started to get mean-spirited, and then I started getting mean-spirited back. I told him that I just might have a nice long talk with Janet and tell her what her sweet husband has been up to for the last four years. Vernon got really pissed-off then and told me that if I so much as spoke a word to Janet he would wring my neck."

Carla started to cry then and tried to continue her story while her eyes overflowed. "I just couldn't believe he was talking to me like that. All we shared and everything we did, and we did some pretty crazy stuff. You know, Vernon has been involved in some shady things over the years, and while I don't think he would really do anything to hurt me, he sure scared the crap out of me tonight."

"You know, he's really a good lookin' man; he's tall and built real nice. He has wavy black hair and his eyes are usually brown and gentle, but tonight his eyes looked dark and mean and so hateful. I never seen him like that. So I told him to just go to hell and that I quit and walked out and slammed the damn door. So now I'm out of a job and don't have Vernon anymore. My life sure sucks, Chris, and here I am looking like Frankenstein and my face hurts like fire. Am I a winner or what?"

"Carla, I'm so sorry. I know how much you cared for him. I don't know what to say."

"You know, I don't know either."

"So what brought on the fight with Frankie? Did he find out about Vernon or what happened?"

"Well, that's another story. After I left the restaurant, I stopped in a bar on the way home and had a couple of drinks. I really needed them, Chris; I was so upset. Maybe I had a few more than a couple, but I was listening to the music and talking to some of the guys there and having a good time and just trying to forget about this mess with Vernon, and time just went by. You know how that is, right?"

"When I left, this one guy, Stony—I think he lives in the apartments because I seen him around before, well, this guy asks if he can walk me home, and I just laughed and said that I walked home from work at night for years now, and I'll be okay. He said, 'Be careful now, pretty girl,' and that made me feel good."

"Then I started out, it's only a three-block walk. So, I'm walking along and something didn't feel right. So I look around and there's that guy Terry, I told you about him. He's the liquor store guy. Well, Terry is only a few steps behind me. He must have followed me out of the bar. I didn't see him in the bar. He probably was sitting in a corner or somewhere dark because I don't remember seeing him. If I had I would have probably let Stony walk me home. Anyway, he's got this shitty grin on his face and says, 'Hey, sweet cheeks, wait up for your ole' friend Terry.' "

"I started walking faster and so did he. He caught up to me and grabbed me by my arm. I'll tell you, Chris, he smelled so bad, like week-old garbage, and when he smiled and showed his yellow, slimy teeth I almost puked. I pulled my arm away and said, 'Hi, Terry. Got to get home, talk to you another time.' "

"He said, 'Maybe you want some company. The store is just a few blocks away and we can have a nightcap—just you and me.' I told him no thanks and started to run. He was right behind me so I stopped and turned around and told him to get lost and he said, 'You owe me, you stupid bitch, all that wine I let you walk out with—now it's payback time.' "

I told him, in I guess a nasty way, that he was the last man on earth that I would ever let touch me and some other things I probably shouldn't have said, but I did anyway and meant them. He made a grab for me then and ripped my sleeve. I kneed him in the balls and took off running. I ran all the way home. I don't think he followed me. I didn't look behind me I just ran like hell."

"Oh, my God, not that man, that creepy guy. You poor thing, you must have been so scared."

Carla tapped the heel of her hand on her forehead

and said, "Well, duh, what do you think, I almost peed myself. I was never so glad to see this hellhole building in all my life. I was shaking so hard I could hardly push the button on the elevator. I sure wasn't going to use the stairs. And the rest I told you. I opened the door and there sat Mr. Wonderful waiting for me."

"You know, Chris, my life really sucks right now, no job, no Vernon, an asshole for a husband, and I'm pretty sure no more free wine from Terry, and look at me. Frankie has hit me before but never this bad. What the hell am I going to do? If it weren't for my boys, I'd be outta here. Don't know where I'd go, but I'd be outta here quicker than you could say—Oh hell who am I kidding, I'm stuck."

Chris didn't know what to say to console Carla. She herself was shaking from all this drama and violence. And the very thought of that pervert Terry grabbing at Carla made her stomach roll.

Both women sat on the couch too tired to talk or get up. It was now almost 5:00. Finally, Carla pushed herself up off the couch and announced that she was going home. She said she knew Frankie would be asleep by now and she had to wake the boys for school in two hours. Chris walked her to the door and they embraced for a long while and Carla left thanking Chris for all her help.

Chris made herself crawl into bed and lay awake until exhaustion took over. She was in the midst of a dark depressing dream of some sort when the alarm rang out. It was 7:15 and time to get everyone moving.

It amazed her that the children had not heard a thing last night. But no one said anything and she didn't bring it up. After they got off to school, she took Wittles out and then went to work.

Chapter 46

Her job as a receptionist in Dr. Cooper's office was getting more interesting. He gave her additional responsibilities that gave her a feeling of accomplishment and satisfaction. As he discovered just how intelligent she was, he increased her duties and salary little by little hoping to keep her in his employment. Chris had been able to put an occasional small amount of money aside, for her getaway just in case they had to move out because of Wittles. This gave her a very secure feeling. She knew they would go on to a better apartment eventually, but things were going pretty good for her and the children right now so she had decided to take advantage of the low rent for awhile and keep saving for the future.

Over the years, she always had hopes of continuing her nursing career. Working with doctors and nurses made her want it even more. One time she had a conversation with Sylvia, an RN in one of the building's medical offices, and Sylvia gave her advice on which schools in the area were more affordable and how to apply. Apparently there was a wait to get into the schools, so Sylvia encouraged Chris to get on a waiting list somewhere soon.

Within a week, she had found an acceptable school and had her name put on the waiting list. Chris was disappointed that nothing from her one year of college would transfer. It had been too long. So here she was at

38, trying to start her career over again. She felt frustrated but at the same time she felt fortunate that her dream was at least a possibility.

Chapter 47

As hard as it was to see their old home, Chris' family occasionally visited with Laura and Don and their children. The visits were less and less as the months went by, but the friendships still endured. Becky, Bobby, and Scott would spend some time with their old neighbors and then would head out to look up some old school friends. Chris worried at first that it would make the kids too nostalgic for times gone by, but being kids, they adjusted pretty well. On all of their visits, Chris held a shivering Wittles on her lap. If she tried to put her down, she would cry and try to climb back. She wondered if it wouldn't be better leaving Wittles at the apartment, but hoped she would eventually get over her fear of being at Laura's house.

Most visits Chris would sit at Laura's kitchen table and talk away just like they used to do. Sometimes Don would join them. It was very comforting for Chris because she had made no new friends since she had moved except for Carla and Mrs. Weber. One afternoon Chris mentioned that she had applied to a nursing school and was now on a waiting list. She asked Don if he knew anything about student aid or loans, and Don, being the kindhearted man that he was, said he would do some investigating for Chris and get back to her as soon as he could.

They all loved their visits, seeing good friends, having a dinner all together, laughing at crazy things the kids had done or the parties they had gone to or hosted.

The only bad part of going back to Penn St. was seeing their beautiful home and noticing some of the changes that had been made. Shortly after they moved in, the new owners had replaced Chris' huge American Beauty rosebush that had been a centerpiece in the front yard. Chris had treated that rosebush with tender loving care for years. It produced roses that were the reddest and largest in the whole neighborhood. Laura said that one day it was just gone and in its place was an empty space that had been planted with grass seed. Apparently, someone didn't like roses or maybe was allergic. Oh well, Chris figured, they can do what they want with it now. The house had provided her family many happy memories and a lot of memories she would rather forget.

Chapter 48

Three days had gone by now without seeing Carla. She didn't even show up for their nightly meetings with Precious and Wittles. Chris was starting to get worried. All kinds of ideas were going over and over in her head. Maybe Frankie had hit her again and she was ashamed to be seen or he had hurt her really bad. Maybe she was afraid to go out because of that creep Terry. Maybe she was heartsick about Vernon breaking up with her and losing her job.

Finally, when the worry got the better of her, Chris went next door to Carla's apartment and knocked. She had never been in Carla's apartment, mainly because she had never been invited.

There were no sounds coming from the inside. This seemed strange since there were five people and a dog living there and usually Chris could hear voices or the television. After waiting for what seemed like forever, Chris wished she hadn't come and decided to just go back to her place. As she turned to go, the door opened and there stood Frankie. Chris gulped and tried not to show her distaste and fear of the man.

Chris had only seen Frankie a few times in the months they had lived here. At those times she had only caught glimpses of him. He was a thin man, not very tall, probably only a few inches taller than Carla, and she was no more than five feet. He had dark, balding hair and was wearing a sleeveless white T-shirt and baggy gray sweatpants. Chris took a step backwards when he almost yelled, "Well, what do you want?"

The smell of alcohol and something else, maybe garlic, poured forth from his mouth along with his unwelcoming words. She just stared at him a second wondering what to say. Finally, getting up her courage she asked if she could speak to Carla.

"You can speak to her if you can find her. The bitch took off, and I ain't heard from her in three days. I thought she was staying with you since the boy here told me you're the only one she ever talks to around here. Can you imagine, she just left and didn't come home? She left me here with these damned kids to take care of and feed. I never cooked in my life. My mother, bless her soul, always cooked for her husband and kids every day of her life. She would never have run out on us. She was a saint. She wasn't like Carla—the stupid bitch."

If Chris had disliked him before, she definitely loathed him now. "Well, Frankie, aren't you worried about her? Have you reported her missing? She told me that she has no family around here. She hasn't contacted me, and I can't imagine she would leave the kids for so long."

"Lady, I'm done talking. Here, talk to the boy. Victor, come here and you gossip with our noisy neighbor here. I'm a busy man and I ain't got no time for all this chit-chatting bullshit."

Before Chris could open her mouth in her defense, Frankie turned and disappeared into another room. Two seconds later, Victor appeared. He looked rather sheepish and tried to apologize for his father's rudeness.

Chris tried to put him at ease. "Hey, Victor, I understand. How are you and your brothers doing?"

"Okay, I guess. Well, really not okay. We're pretty worried about Mom. She has never done this before. We're all really hungry and all there is to eat is a bag of stale potato chips. Dad says he doesn't have any money, so we're screwed. Mrs. Cunningham, where do you think Mom went?"

"Victor, start from the beginning. When did she leave? What day?"

"It was three days ago—probably around 8:00 at night. Dad was being real mean again so she said she had to get out of here for a while. She put on her coat and took her purse and left. Dad started to follow her but came back in a few minutes because he said it was too cold outside. He said he didn't know where the hell she was going. Sorry about the swear, Mrs. Cunningham, his words."

"Three days ago, wasn't that the night of the blizzard?"

"Yeah, it was terrible out."

Chris remembered that day. It was the coldest day of the year and a blizzard was in full swing. She had taken Wittles out in the evening, and she and the dog were almost blown away by the strong wind. They had stayed close to the building and came in quickly because the snow was so heavy. The visibility was close to zero. It was one of those days that had been impossible to stay warm. The frigid air blew through the cracks in the windows, and they all had to put on extra sweaters and wrapped themselves in blankets.

"You know, I thought Mom was probably staying at

your place, but when I asked Bobby the next morning while we were waiting for the bus, he said Mom hadn't been there. Dad just said to forget it, that she'll come back when she's good and ready. But me and Tony and Joey are worried. Dad's being a real jerk, don't seem like he cares if she ever comes home. Do you think she's okay—do you think she'll be back soon?"

Victor was close to tears and Chris gave him a quick hug. "I don't know what to tell you, honey. Let's hope she's all right and is staying with someone for a few days, but until we know for sure, don't you think it's best to call the police and report her as missing?"

Victor's face brightened, "Yes, please, please do that. I've tried to get Dad to call, but like I said, he's being a real jerk. He said he would kick my ass, I mean butt, sorry, if me or my brothers called."

Chris thought a moment and then asked Victor to get his father again. It took about two minutes until 'his majesty' finally appeared.

"Frankie, I'd like to take the boys back to my apartment for a little while and fix them a good meal. Victor said they were all pretty hungry. If you agree, I'll be sure to send something back for you to eat."

"Hey, take them all, keep them if you want. I'm sick of this whole bunch. A wife who runs out on you and three crybaby boys, whining that they miss their mama and that they're hungry all the time. God-almighty how's a man supposed to deal with all this? I wish I could just leave like that crazy wife of mine. That's what I should do—just leave. I would too if I had somewhere to go."

Frankie took a big swallow out of his beer bottle, spilling some of if on his already stained T-shirt. "Hey, I got an idea." He laughed a lecherous laugh. "Why don't I move in with you, sweetie?" He laughed and laughed at his joke and then disappeared again.

Chris uttered a sound of disgust. She wondered how he had money for beer when he couldn't feed his own children. She gathered up all three boys before Frankie changed his mind and took the hungry bunch back to her apartment. They were all good-looking children with their dark hair and brown eyes. They looked so much alike except for the range of heights, like stair steps.

Chris' kids were delighted to have the Carbella boys visit. There had always been friends over when they lived on Penn St., but no one had been over for a meal since they had moved, except Mrs. Weber.

Chris scooted the whole bunch of them into the living room where they could talk and watch TV while she prepared a huge meatloaf and piles of mashed potatoes. She fixed a big, healthy salad and decided on chocolate ice cream and peanut butter cookies for dessert.

As the smell of the meatloaf started to permeate the room, the children gravitated towards the kitchen and sat at the table until dinner was ready. Carla's boys ate like they were starving, which they probably were. Chris' own kids didn't do bad either. When the meal was finished, there was not a morsel left for Frankie, so Chris made him a peanut butter and jelly sandwich. Too bad, that would have to do, she thought, and smiled as she put the sandwich in a brown paper bag. Then because she was in a generous mood, she added one cookie.

After some thought, Chris decided to give Frankie one more chance to report his missing wife. If he wouldn't, she would. So with the kids eating their dessert, watching a Seinfeld rerun, she grabbed the brown lunch bag and knocked on the door again. She knocked for almost a minute until Frankie appeared. Chris handed him the bag and he looked confused.

"What the hell is this and what are you doing back here again?"

Chris pointed to the bag and said, "This is the dinner I promised you."

Frankie opened the sack and took out the sandwich. Chris expected him to be really angry but he actually seemed pleased, especially when he saw the cookie.

"Hey, thanks, neighbor. You're not so bad after all." And giving Chris a stupid-looking wink he said, "Why don't you come on in, the wife and kids aren't home."

Chris took a few steps back and said, "Knock it off, Frankie. I want you to know that I've decided that if you don't report Carla missing, I'm going to."

Again Frankie surprised her when he said, "You can call if you want to. I'm not calling nobody because the hell with her. She wanted to leave and that's okay with me. I say good riddance. I just wish she'd have taken the boys with her. I'm sick of them all. A good man can't get anything done around here, there is always something."

Chris said, "I'm going to call the police now. I had debated whether to wait until morning, but if Carla is in some kind of danger, it's best to call right away."

Frankie nodded. "Do what you want, sister. I don't give a crap one way or another."

Chris started to leave but turned around, "Let me give you some advice. When I call, I'm sure someone will come here this evening to talk to you. It might be wise get rid of the beer and have yourself a few cups of strong coffee. And for goodness sake, put on a clean shirt. Don't you think that would be wise?"

"Hey, who the hell do you think you are, lady? Don't you try and tell me what to do."

Chris added, "Oh, it might also be good to let the boys stay with me tonight. That way they won't be exposed to all the anxiety of having the police here and all the questions. If they are needed for anything, they'll be right next door."

Frankie laughed, "Boy, lady, you're a bossier bitch than my old lady. Hell, keep them for the night. Keep them period. You think you don't have enough kids? Women! What a bunch of losers." He slammed the door.

Chris slowly shook her head. "Oh, Carla, I knew he was a worm but I didn't know just how bad he was." As she walked back to her apartment, she said a silent prayer for Carla. "Please God, let her be safe and somewhere warm."

Six heads turned as Chris walked in and headed for the phone. Victor came and stood next to her while she dialed the police station.

"I guess Dad didn't want to call the police himself, huh? Did he think she was all right or just didn't care?"

"I'm sure your father cares, Victor, but he's in a bad mood right now, so I'm going to call." Chris wasn't sure what was the right thing to say, and she surely didn't want to tell the boys what she really thought of their dad.

When the operator answered, Chris matter-of-factly informed them about Carla's disappearance. The operator asked a few questions and then asked for her address. Chris gave them her address and Frankie's address and was told that someone would be out as soon as possible.

The tension was noticeably building as they waited for the police to arrive. Finally, after about forty minutes of no one talking, just pretending to watch TV, Chris heard some commotion in the hall and a loud knock on the apartment next door.

In a feeble attempt to ease everyone's nervousness, Chris went to the kitchen and got out a bag of pretzels and some Kool-Aid and sat the snacks on the kitchen table. Kids being kids, they were somewhat distracted for a short while. Then Joey walked into the bathroom, shut the door, and started to cry. Victor went after him and tried to console him, while Tony sat stone-faced at the kitchen table slowly eating one pretzel stick after another. Chris' own children, not knowing what to do, went back into the living room and sat quietly together on the sofa.

Chris followed her kids into the living room. She sat on a footstool facing them and said, "This is a difficult time for Carla's boys and I know for us too. I am hopeful that the police will find Carla and that she'll be safely home soon. But for tonight I think it's best if the boys stay here. In the morning, they can go home and get ready for school.

Becky nodded, "Mom, Victor said that his dad is a drunk and they are really afraid of him."

"I know, Becky, that's why I want them here for the night."

Soon they heard the door closing next door and almost immediately there was a knock on Chris' door. Everyone quickly stood up and looked at Chris for instructions. She told them to all sit in the living room and she would handle the situation. When they were all seated, Chris opened the door. There were two police officers, one male and one female, standing in the hall. They showed their badges and introduced themselves as Officers Manor and Lynch. Chris invited them to sit at the kitchen table and they proceeded with the questioning.

"Mrs. Cunningham, your neighbor, Mr. Carbella stated that you are his wife's best friend and the only friend that she has, that he knows about."

"Yes, I am her friend. I don't think she has any other friends, but I can't be certain of that."

The female officer, Officer Lynch, said, "Mr. Carbella also stated that his sons, Victor, Anthony, and Joseph are here with you and we need to question them, but first we'd like to ask you a few questions."

Chris nodded.

"Okay then, we also understand that you called our station to report Mrs. Carbella as a missing person. What makes you think that, Mrs. Cunningham?"

"Well, usually I see her everyday when we take our dogs out in the evening, but I haven't seen her for four or five days now. We've had some really bad weather, you know, and I assumed she didn't want to go out."

"What finally precipitated your going to the Carbella's apartment to inquire about Mrs. Carbella?"

Well, like I said, it just seemed odd that I hadn't seen her for so long and I was worried about her."

"Was there any particular reason, except for the bad weather, that makes you worried about her? Anything that you can think of that you might consider strange or unusual that happened prior to the last time you saw Mrs. Carbella? Anything at all?"

"Well, it just seemed strange that I haven't seen her—like I said, I usually see her everyday and I was worried about her."

"Was there any particular reason your were worried about Mrs. Carbella?"

"Well, the last time I saw Carla—it was Friday, I think, she was very upset."

"What was she upset about?"

"She had an argument with Mr. Carbella and…"

Just then Victor got up and quickly walked into the kitchen. "You guys don't need to be asking Mrs. Cunningham that. You should be talking to me. I was there. Hey, my dad hit my mom, okay? He fell down because he was so drunk and then grabbed her legs before she could get away and pulled her down. He hit her bunches of times and me and my brothers had to jump on him till Mom got away. She was all bloody and scared and stuff. I'll bet the big bully never told you any of that, did he?" The words had poured from Victor with such fury, an explosive release of many years of fear and frustration.

Officer Manor was writing very quickly on his pad of paper, trying to get all of this information written down. "Mr. Carbella said they had a disagreement, but no violence was mentioned."

"Well, that's what happened. Ask Mrs. C. Mom came over here didn't she, Mrs. C? She was all bloody, wasn't she? Tell them I'm not making any of this up."

"Yes," Chris said, "What Victor said is true and

everything coincides with what Carla told me that evening."

The questioning went on for a little while longer. The police excluded questioning the younger boys about what happened in their home. After the questioning, Officer Lynch said, "Mrs. Cunningham, a detective from our department will want to talk to you about this case, if Mrs. Carbella doesn't come home soon. Do you have any objections to that?" Chris answered, "Of course not, officer. Your department can contact me any time."

When the officers went back to talk to Frankie, Chris went about finding places for everyone to sleep for the night.

Chapter 49

A block away from the apartments, the snow was piled high, higher in many places where the wind had blown the snow into big drifts almost to the top of a rusty, dilapidated fence. After a time, the once pristine and fluffy snow had hardened and was dotted with all kinds of debris frozen in its midst. There was a small patch of trees nearby with thin bare limbs that looked like black arms grabbing for the sky. It was there, just two days after Chris reported Carla missing, five days after Carla had left during the storm, that an elderly man who was walking his old German Shepherd discovered Carla's body. The big dog ran from its owner and pawed at the snow-covered form. When the dog uncovered a frozen hand, the man almost fainted from the horror and hurried to find help.

Everyone was so shocked. Carla's boys were not to be consoled, and even Frankie seemed to be grieving. Chris cried and cried for her friend and prayed that Carla was finally happy, safe, and warm in Heaven.

Carla's body was removed to the morgue for an autopsy. The results were pending when Detective Spencer Simmons visited Chris. He was a big man who somewhat resembled her father. He had dark hair and kind blue eyes. He quietly asked Chris the question she had been dreading. "Do you know of anyone who could have harmed Carla? Did she tell you anything that might help us in our investigation?"

Chris had known she would eventually have to answer that question. She was all alone in this world, trying to protect her teenaged daughter and two sons, and she knew that answering the question honestly could put them all in harm's way. Ever since Carla's body was found, she had struggled with what she would say, she had prayed for guidance, and when she answered the detective's question she felt she must tell the worst lie she had ever told. She said "no."

After the authorities released Carla's body, Frankie stated that he wasn't going to have a funeral for his wife. He said that Carla wouldn't want a bunch of nosy people gawking at her dead body.

Chris had to agree that Carla wouldn't like that at all, but the simple truth was Frankie didn't have the money. They had no insurance or savings; he was broke. The money Carla earned working part-time at Vernon's restaurant along with a small sum from welfare was the only income the family had.

Frankie's older sister, Sophie, stepped in and insisted that they should at least have a memorial service with closed coffin at a local non-denominational church. Frankie agreed when she offered to pay the bill. Sophie had little regard for her brother, but she had always liked Carla and their sons.

After the funeral, Carla's boys and their dog were whisked away to live with their Aunt Sophie in Newark. Sophie was determined that her nephews would never have a decent life if they were raised by her brother. Frankie put up a weak argument, but he was really quite relieved. Sophie told him that if and when he ever got his life together, stopped drinking, and got a job, they would talk about an arrangement for him to get his boys back.

Frankie packed up and left shortly after that. He packed up a few boxes and was gone. Rumor on the fourth floor had it that he left most of the furniture and other things and just disappeared. Chris never saw or heard from Frankie or the boys again.

The local newspaper indicated that the dead woman was intoxicated and had probably wandered away in the storm and froze to death. There was no mention of any foul play. Detective Simmons reiterated this on his next visit. He gave her his card and told her to call for any reason. Chris was so relieved. She had been wrestling with her conscience and was about to tell Detective Simmons what she knew about Vernon and Terry. But with this new information Chris didn't feel the need to say anything further.

Chapter 50

March and April came and went without any drama. Chris was doing well with her job, the kids were continuing to adjust, and there were no more hassles from Mrs. Gallagher. The latter was partially due to Mrs. Weber, the sweet elderly lady who lived across the hall. Chris had given her a key to her apartment, and Mrs. Weber checked on Wittles every day and sometimes took the dog back to her home where she spoiled her along with her old cat. In appreciation, Chris invited Mrs. Weber for dinner often.

Chapter 51

It was very unusual for the telephone to ring at 7:30 on a Sunday morning. Chris awoke with a start and quickly grabbed the phone. A small, shaky voice asked to speak to Christine Cunningham. She said her name was Dora Douglas and that she was a good friend of Paulette Cunningham.

"Yes, Dora, this is Christine. What can I do for you?"

"Well, actually, Christine, Paulette is in the hospital. Seems like she has a problem with her heart, and I didn't know who else to call seeing as how her son isn't, well....available right now. I thought maybe, at least I hoped, you can help her out because she is scheduled to come home from the hospital in two days and well, I'm not in good health myself." Dora's voice broke as she struggled to continue. "Like I said, I didn't know who else to call. I know you and Paulette don't get along, but, well…"

Chris cut in and said, "Calm down, Dora, of course I will help. Did she have a heart attack or stroke? How long has she been in the hospital? When did this happen? Is she going to be all right? Gosh, I don't know what to say, but of course we will help her in any way we can. Thank you for calling, Dora, and for helping Paulette."

Chris heard a big sigh at the other end of the line. "Thank you, Christine, thank you."

They talked for a while longer, and Dora answered all of Chris' questions. She told her that Paulette did have a heart attack, but was resting comfortably and that she had been taken to the hospital yesterday morning. Paulette had called her and told her she wasn't feeling well and Dora called 911 and followed the ambulance to the hospital. The call ended with a promise to Dora to go see her ex-mother-in-law that afternoon.

When Chris and the children visited Paulette later that day, she assured Paulette that she would help her with her recovery. Paulette was uncharacteristically mild and seemed relieved if not happy to see them all. Chris took off work for two days so she and the children could stay with Paulette her first two days at home. Chris then arranged for a nursing service to provide twenty-four hour care for her as long as it was needed. Paulette put up a fuss about the expense, but she was adamant about not going to a nursing home for her rehabilitation, and she definitely had the resources to be able to afford private care.

It took six weeks before Paulette was able to take care of herself. Her heart attack had left her weak but able to do most things for herself after her recovery period. Chris continued to visit her as much as she could, and their once caustic relationship seemed to dissipate more with each visit. Paulette started to become the loving grandmother that Becky, Bobby, and Scott had hoped for. They all started to be comfortable with each other, and sometimes laughter could be heard from the quiet, dark house for the first time in many years.

From the first day, Chris wanted to inform Ted of his mother's condition, but Paulette insisted that her son was going through such an ordeal she didn't want to add to his worry. It was hard for Chris to believe that almost nine months had gone by and they all had survived and were doing so well, despite everything that had happened.

Chapter 52

"Look to your right, head down a little—somebody blot her upper lip." Lisa wanted to tear off the heavy jacket and slacks that she was wearing. The hot New York sun glared down unmercifully, and the shoot that had gone on for over an hour seemed like it would never end. Lisa envied the photographer and his crew wearing their T-shirts, shorts, and sandals. She wondered whose bright idea it was to shoot a winter layout in 90-degree weather. Just when she felt like she would pass out from the heat, the photographer decreed that he was finished and she could leave. Swearing under her breath, she went back to the trailer to change.

After peeling off the sodden jacket and slacks, Lisa gabbed a bottle of water from the refrigerator, switched on the air-conditioner, and plopped down on the sofa wearing only her very skimpy underwear.

The air conditioner was making sounds like a plane taking off. She couldn't hear the door open and close, so she didn't realize she was not alone until Burt Quinn walked toward her. Burt was the CEO of the modeling agency where she was working today. He quickly sat down next to Lisa, very close, and gave her bare leg a playful slap. "Hey, babe, lookin' good out there today—and lookin' damn good in here. Look what I brought you, sweetheart?" Burt held up a six-pack of beer.

Lisa quickly scooted to the other side of the sofa,

grabbing a pillow to hold against her. "Come on, Burt, you need to get out of here. This trailer is off-limits to men, you know that."

"Calm down, little lady, I just thought you might want a nice cold beer and a little company. It's hot as hell out there."

"There's beer in the refrigerator, and I just need some time to cool off, and I sure don't want any company. Now get moving, Burt."

Burt got up part way, as if to leave, then shifted his rear to sit next to Lisa again. His large body flopped rather than sat down. His once handsome face, now unattractively craggy, along with his combed-over dyed black hair and bloodshot blue eyes, did nothing to help him as he tried to look sexy and appealing. It was sickeningly obvious by his manner and breath that he had been drinking—a lot. With his face just a few inches from Lisa's, he clumsily grabbed at her and tried to pull her toward him.

Lisa reacted quickly and pushed him back with all her might. When he wouldn't budge, she raised both feet and with sheer determination, shoved the big drunken man away from her.

"Get the hell away from me, Burt, you creep," Lisa said as she got up and started walking toward the bedroom.

Burt was not taking no for an answer, however, and he got up swiftly and pulled Lisa to the floor. His large body quickly blanketed hers and pinned her to the cold tile. He started pulling at her bra strap and revealed a bare breast. Lisa was so furious she hit Burt in the nose as hard as she could and rolled out from under him. She quickly made it to the bedroom and locked the door while Burt was holding his nose and screaming in pain.

From the safety of the locked door, Lisa yelled, "You'd better leave now or I'm calling security."

Lisa threw on her robe and went to listen by the door. She heard some stumbling and grumbling, then the opening and closing of the trailer's door. She cautiously opened the bedroom door and peeked out to see if he had really left. Once sure that he was gone, she ran to the trailer's door and locked it.

Burt must have changed his mind because as soon as the lock clicked, there he was trying to open the door and loudly cursing Lisa. His face was red and furious. "I own this goddamned trailer and you're working for me, you little tease—sitting there in nothing but your skimpy underwear. Let me in. I left my beer in there. Let me in, you little bitch. I own this trailer and who do you think signs your paychecks, girl?"

He rattled the door handle a few more times, then still ranting and raving he raised his fist as he slowly staggered away. "You'll never work for me again, do you hear me Miss High and Mighty, never work for me in a million years. I know all about you. You get it on for any man that has enough money. Well, I'm a very, very rich man and you'll be sorry you little tramp. Sorry, that's what you'll be." His voice trailed off as he got further and further away.

Once sure that Burt was gone, Lisa went into the bedroom and sat on the bed. She was shaking almost uncontrollably. She hugged herself tightly in an attempt to calm down, determined not to cry. She was scared but she was also mad as hell. She allowed herself a few minutes to get her composure back and then she called Miranda.

She managed to convey Burt's depraved behavior of the last hour, trying not to forget a word or action. Miranda was very sympathetic but, as always, practical. She told Lisa, "We can handle this situation one of two ways. You can claim sexual harassment in the workplace and ask for a monetary settlement or you can try and forget it ever happened. My recommendation is to forget it."

"Miranda, you can't be serious. Why on earth should I let this go? That crazy drunk tried to rape me."

"Well, Lisa, let's be practical. Thank God he didn't rape you, but if he did you would have more of a leg to stand on to press any kind of charges. You're smart enough to know what Burt will say. He'll deny everything because there were no witnesses, right? He'd more than likely get some of his cronies to say you willingly slept with them, and if I'm not mistaken, you probably have; mind you, I'm not throwing stones or anything. Let's face it, anyway it would end up, in your favor or his, word would get out quickly in this man's business and you would get screwed—figuratively. Not many employers would touch you with a ten-foot pole if you sued one of their own for sexual harassment. You would be unemployable. Get it? Not fair, Lisa, but that's the way it is. So that's why my advice is to swallow your pride and forget it."

"Miranda, that's just not the way it should be. I didn't do anything to egg him on. Why should I be the one to just forget it and let him get away with this kind of inexcusable behavior? It's just not right."

"Honey, you're preaching to the choir. You asked my advice and I think this is what's best for you, if you want to continue in this business. Got to go now. Think this one over carefully and get back to me soon. We'll handle it whichever way you choose."

Lisa slammed down the phone; she was fuming. She wasn't mad at Miranda. She knew Miranda was right but angry because she knew she was whipped, defeated by the 'big boys club'. In this day and age where there was supposedly equality of the sexes, the 'big boys club' was still alive and well and probably would go on forever.

Checking again that the door was still securely locked, Lisa went into the small, cramped shower and shivered under the dinky shower-head until the water turned hot. Then trying to relax, she let the water fall on her tense body hoping it would soothe away all the drama of the day.

When the water turned cool, she dried off and dressed in shorts and a summer T-shirt. Snatching up her cosmetic bag and valise, she left the trailer and rode off in her little red Mercedes to her apartment.

Sometime between the end of the conversation with Miranda and the drive home, Lisa made a huge decision that would affect the rest of her life. She was getting out of the modeling business; she had to. Work was no longer fun; in fact, it sucked big time. She was sick of all the crap that was required to be a success. She simply didn't want to play the game anymore.

If truth be told, this decision wasn't a snap decision. It had consciously or unconsciously been on her mind for a long time, really ever since she left Ted. She had been thinking about Ted a lot lately. Granted, Ted did wrong, but she realized now that he did it for her, just for her. He had loved her enough to take the chances that led him to prison. She had left him high and dry.

Maybe she should have cared less about the money and more about how good they were together and could be again. Maybe she was growing up.

She recently had become more aware of families and children and to her dismay, she rather liked the idea. Also to her dismay, Lisa felt a longing to belong to somebody and have someone belong to her. When she was thinking this way, her thoughts always went back to Ted.

Chapter 53

The next day, after hours of soul searching, Lisa decided to try and find Ted and ask for his forgiveness. She had no idea what prison he was sentenced to, but was determined to find him.

Lisa asked herself where she could begin. She would never call Chris, even if she knew where Chris was. She knew Chris would never tell her a thing after the way she cussed her out before heading to New York. Her only other hope was Ted's mother. Ted had told Lisa that he had talked about their plans with her and she knew the situation. She immediately called information and got Ted's mother's phone number.

She put on her friendliest voice and dialed Mrs. Cunningham before she lost her nerve. The phone rang a long time and just as Lisa was about to hang up, it was answered by a soft, almost weak voice.

Lisa introduced herself to Mrs. Cunningham and politely asked for Ted's address. There was a long pause and then the voice on the other end of the phone got steadily stronger as she said, "Who did you say you are and why do you want to know my son's whereabouts?"

"I am a good friend of Ted's and I'm sure he would like to hear from me."

"How do you know, Ted? You know I just can't give out this information to anyone. Who are you anyway, young lady?"

Lisa swallowed hard. She hadn't expected the conversation to go this way. Ted's mother's voice seemed very unfriendly and confrontational. She took a deep breath and said, "Mrs. Cunningham, I'm Lisa. I know Ted told you about me, about how we were going to be married after his divorce. Of course, you know we didn't get that chance because of his incarceration and all and then we lost touch somehow because I had to go back to work in New York."

"What do you mean that you were going to marry my son? He was already married and has three children. Did you know that? Well, did you? Ted swore to me that there was no other woman. He swore to me. What is this, some kind of prank? You say your name is Lisa, well Lisa, who are you really, and what are you trying to pull, young lady? Who put you up to this? Tell me, I said tell me." Paulette's voice rose with each word until she was almost screaming.

Lisa was getting impatient with the hysterical old lady and started to lose her composure. "Like I said, your son was getting a divorce and then we were going to be married, got it, Grandma?"

"How dare you call me Grandma! I don't know you and I don't believe for a minute that my son would have anything to do with you. He had a lovely wife and three beautiful children, and he swore to me many times, many times that there was no one else. He wouldn't lie to me, he wouldn't. He's a good son. He wouldn't lie about that, not to his mother. You just leave me and my son alone, I..." Suddenly, Paulette felt pain and her heart started thumping again. She hung up the phone with Lisa and quickly dialed 911.

Lisa swore at Ted's mother after she had slammed the phone down loudly. The old bat was really mean. Lisa figured she was probably so feeble she had forgotten when Ted had told her that they were going to be married. It never occurred to her that he had never really told his mother.

Now the problem of locating Ted seemed impossible. She thought for a while and then it hit her that she could get the information in Fremont County, the place where Ted's sentencing most likely took place. She decided to drive there and look up the records.

Chapter 54

As soon as she was settled in her hospital room, Paulette called Chris. Chris was at work but immediately left and went to the hospital. Chris rushed into Paulette's hospital room not knowing what she would find. Paulette was hooked up to several machines and had an oxygen mask to help her breathe. She looked so old and sick, a lot worse than her last stay several weeks ago.

The doctor informed Chris that Paulette had suffered a small attack this time, not as much damage but she needed to stay for a few days for observation.

When Paulette saw Chris she smiled and raised her hand slowly in greeting. Chris sat with her for several hours and when Chris was sure Paulette was resting peacefully she arose to leave and kissed her on the forehead. As she started towards the door, Paulette said, "Chris, please stay."

Chris walked back to Paulette's bed. Paulette removed her oxygen mask and whispered, "Chris, you've been so good to me. I think I've misjudged you. I've been thinking about my son, and I think, you know, I believe now there was another woman. Tell me what you know about her. Please, I know this isn't easy for you, but I need to know. Who was she, Chris? What was her name?"

"Paulette, that's over now. Let's not talk about it while you're so sick, OK? You just rest and get better and we'll talk some other time. Actually, I don't know much about her, just that her name is Lisa."

"Lisa, her name is Lisa." Paulette let out a groan and closed her eyes. Chris stayed a few minutes longer and then quietly left.

Three days later, Paulette went home. Five days after that, she had another heart attack and died.

Chapter 55

Ted was allowed to come home for his mother's funeral. His behavior had been exemplary, and he was allowed a week to bury his mother and settle her affairs.

Although Ted was truly sad about his mother's death, he was tremendously relieved that his money worries would be over. In three months, he was scheduled to be released, and after he received his inheritance, he could do whatever and go wherever he wanted. His mother's estate had to be at least a half-million dollars or maybe more.

When Ted saw Chris and his children after all these months, he was shocked. The kids had grown like weeds, and Chris had a different, rather lean and healthy look. Her appearance was quite appealing. Ted's presence produced reluctant hugs and embarrassed hesitations in conversations with his children. However, after the first day the uneasiness with their father decreased and they all relaxed a bit.

Chris handled Ted's brief visit with polite disinterest. Because of the occasion, she was civil but in no way was he welcomed with open arms.

The funeral itself was quite somber and sparsely attended. Dora and two other friends of Paulette were present along with Ted, Chris, and Paulette's three grandchildren. There were four funeral bouquets standing in the large room. One was from Ted and his children, one from the family attorney, one from Billingly, Inc., and a small bouquet from Chris. Paulette would have been so disappointed with the dismal turnout of her funeral.

Chris surprised herself with her feeling of loss. They had just started to care for this woman who had been so distant and disagreeable for so many years. Now she felt like she had lost a friend and was sorry that her children had lost their only grandparent.

Shortly after the funeral, Ted contacted his mother's lawyer to begin settling her estate. Richard Lyons had been their family attorney for many years. He had to be at least seventy now, and Ted was amazed to learn that Mr. Lyons was still working every day, keeping the same schedule as the younger attorneys.

Ted had decided not to sell his mother's big, sprawling house yet. In three months he would need a place to stay, if only temporarily, while he got his act together. "Who knows," Ted thought, "I may never have to work again." That thought was very appealing to him.

He was surprised when he talked to Mr. Lyons. The lawyer stated that Ted's children and ex-wife would be present for the reading of the will. He figured of course his mother would leave something to the kids and Chris being their guardian should be there. He couldn't wait to get this over with. The waiting was making him very nervous.

Ted arrived early for their 2:30 appointment, and Chris and the children came soon afterward.

Ted thought that Mr. Lyons gave him a strange look, almost sheepish, when he directed him where to sit at the long, highly polished cherry conference table. When everyone was in their seat, water and coffee were offered. As there were no takers, the reading began.

Mr. Lyons began by telling his audience that Mrs. Cunningham had called him to her home shortly after she was released from the hospital, only three days before her death. "At that meeting," Mr. Lyons stated, "Mrs. Cunningham changed her will."

Ted started to perspire. His heart started to beat faster and a throbbing headache quickly ensued. He was sure this could not be a good thing. As he tried to calm himself, Mr. Lyons continued.

"I, Paulette R. Cunningham, being of sound mind and body do hereby bequeath all my worldly possessions as follows…" Paulette had left each of her grandchildren one-hundred thousand dollars with Mr. Lyons as trustee, and she gave her home, all contents, and eighty-thousand dollars to Chris, another fifty-thousand was divided up between several of her favorite charities. The remaining monies along with his late father's watch and antique car were left to her son, Theodore. Ted's inheritance amounted to about forty-thousand dollars.

Ted was almost in shock as he listened to Mr. Lyons. When the reading was over, he stood up and proclaimed, "This is an outrage. My mother was a sick woman and she was definitely not in her right mind when she rewrote her will. Richard, I can't believe that you would rewrite a will for someone who was definitely not able to make such decisions. This is bullshit, just plain bullshit. You know my mother would never do this to me. I'm going to fight this in court. This is an outrage, and you all know it." Then, looking over at Chris he said, "What did you do to my mother to get her to do this? What kind of stunt did you pull here, Chris?"

Before Chris could defend herself, Mr. Lyons walked over to Ted and handed him an envelope, "Your mother said if you had any questions, you should read this, Ted." Ted grabbed the envelope and ripped it open. Inside was only a single piece of paper. There were just two sentences that were definitely written in his mother's handwriting. The sentences simply said, "If you try to change my will, you will get nothing. You lied to me, Ted. Her name is Lisa."

Ted took the letter and crushed it in his hands and threw it across the room. Red-faced with anger and humiliation, he grabbed his briefcase and practically ran out of the room saying, "You people haven't heard the last of this. My mother would never do this to me. She loved me. She wouldn't do this."

Chris and the children just stood there during this outburst. Chris didn't know if her kids comprehended what had just happened. She didn't understand it herself. Why would Paulette almost disinherit her only son? Why would she be so generous to her and her children? She looked at Mr. Lyons with questioning eyes.

Mr. Lyons responded by slowly walking across the room and picking up the crumpled note from Paulette that Ted had thrown just a few minutes ago. As he handed it to Chris he said, "You might as well read this. Mrs. Cunningham told me the whole story. That's why she changed her will. I told her there would be trouble from Ted, but she was quite adamant about it, and as I felt she was in complete control of her faculties at the time, I did as she requested."

Chris read the note and gasped, "Oh, my gosh, I can't believe this."

"What is it, Mom? What did Grandma write?" Becky asked, trying to get a look at the paper Chris held.

Chris quickly folded the note. She insisted that the children wait in the reception area while she and Mr. Lyons talked. They reluctantly did as they were asked, knowing that their mother was in no mood to argue.

When Chris and Mr. Lyons were alone, Chris started to cry. "I can't believe that just by telling Paulette a woman's name would cause all this. I'm grateful and all for her generous gifts to my children and myself, but I feel like I've done something wrong here. She did ask me about Ted's girlfriend when she was in the hospital, and I told her I didn't want to talk about it. But when she asked for her name, I did tell Paulette her name. Mr. Lyons, you've got to believe me, I had no thought that by telling her Lisa's name anything like this would result. I should be feeling good, but I feel terrible."

Mr. Lyons smiled and motioned for Chris to sit down. As he handed her a box of tissues he said, "Please, please, Chris, relax. You surely aren't aware of all the circumstances that precipitated the changing of Mrs. Cunningham's will." He then proceeded to relay the story of Lisa's and Paulette's phone conversation and Ted's history with his parents.

"Mrs. Cunningham and her husband had been clients and friends of mine for a long time. I know how much she tried to love her son all these years. But I also know that he was not a good son to her in many ways. All of Ted's life she defended him and managed to get him out of numerous scrapes; she required my assistance in a legal sense more than a few times. I truly think the information she gained from the phone call from the infamous Lisa was what we sometimes call the straw that broke the camel's back."

Mr. Lyons put his hand on Chris' shoulder trying to comfort her as he continued. "Chris, you did nothing wrong. These past few months you have been so helpful and loving to your ex-mother-in-law, and she told me how much she regretted being so distant to you and her grandchildren for so long. She wanted to do something for all of you. This was her decision; this is what she wanted. I know we are going to get a lot of threats from Ted, but it is in Mrs. Cunningham's will that if anyone tries to contest her last wishes, they won't receive a dime. Her will and last wishes are legal and binding, and I'm sure once Ted calms down, he will do nothing to contest his mother's will."

That evening, Chris lay in bed thinking of the events of the day. She was still tying to grasp the enormity of what had transpired at the lawyer's office. Unable to sleep, she got up and wondered around the little apartment stopping to stare out of the small, smudged kitchen window where she could scan the parking lot and the numerous high-rise apartment buildings that seem to cover the horizon.

It was slowly sinking in that her family could now move into a real house. She would no longer be fearful of having enough money to pay the rent, having money for groceries, clothes, and other necessities. The kids would have funds for college, and there would be no more feeling degraded about someone telling her what she could and could not do. And there would be no more anxiety as to when Mrs. Gallagher would find out about Wittles.

She couldn't help but feel sorry for the people who were doomed to live here forever. These people who would never have a house and money just given to them, enabling their getaway from overcrowding and poverty. It had not been quite a year since Chris and her family had moved here. Every day Chris had prayed for an opportunity to leave. She had worked hard, played by all the rules (except for Wittles), and accepted her neighbors and they had accepted her. But the whole time she had lived with fear, fear that if just one thing would go wrong, it could result in their world being turned upside down or worse. It was such a relief to feel secure again.

Chapter 56

Mr. Lyons had apparently been right because no word had been heard from Ted. The lawyer handled all aspects of the will, and in a little over three weeks he had managed to arrange for the final exchange of the house and all monies.

After Chris signed many forms, Mr. Lyons gave her the deed to the house and handed her the keys. Mr. Lyons had arranged to join Chris at a later date with a financial adviser to help her determine what would be the best investments for herself and her children.

She smiled as she left his office and held the keys tightly. It was a pleasant day in June, and the sun was shining brightly. Her mood matched the day. Chris decided to drive to Paulette's house and look over her new home. The kids were in their final week of the school year, so she took this opportunity to examine the house on her own.

Once at the house, she walked up the steps to the sprawling porch feeling a bit intimidated. This old yellow house was her home now, and even after almost a month of knowing this, she still couldn't fully believe it. She slowly looked around the neighborhood reveling in the fact that they would be living in a real neighborhood where there were sidewalks, trees, backyards, and neighbors whose homes were close by, but far enough away that conversations and arguments could not be heard during the day and especially in the middle of the night.

The key fit into the lock easily and the door opened with a loud groan. Once inside, the oppressive scent of roses filled her nostrils. It reminded Chris of a funeral parlor. She closed the door and walked into the living room. It was gloomy and shadows spread in long gray paths throughout the room even though it was still morning.

Chris turned on every light she could find and proceeded to open the drapes. She could not remember one time in her memory of her visits here when the drapes had been opened. The room had always been dark and somewhat ominous. The cord that opened the drapes slowly dragged the heavy material open, protesting with every inch. Once open, it was amazing how bright the room became even though the windows looked as if they had not been cleaned in a very long time. The admittance of the light made the room's contents look worn and shabby, and the walls clearly showed a need for fresh paint.

Chris walked throughout the house, opening all the curtains and drapes, discovering the same neglect in each room. She thought back to when Ted's father was alive. Surely the house had not looked like this. Actually, Chris couldn't remember too much about that time; Ted's father had died shortly after they were married. She did remember that her mother and father-in-law entertained quite often, socializing mostly with people from Billingly. She and her children had never been invited for one meal in seventeen years, although Ted used to stop by for dinner now and then. A hurtful feeling still existed somewhere deep down inside, but she pushed it away. Things were different now. She had forgiven Paulette all her slights, and they had finally become friends.

As she roamed around the house, she felt like an interloper. She had never seen some of the rooms before, only the living room, dining room, kitchen, and downstairs bathroom in all the time she had been married to Ted. The rooms in the house were very organized and decorated plainly. But Chris had a shock when she checked out the attic, basement, and garage. These areas were filled with boxes, old furniture, various bookshelves and cabinets, several old chests, tools, etc. In the garage was Ted's father's antique car, an old Chevrolet, just waiting for Ted to claim it when he was released.

Chris smiled as she remembered some of the books she had read where various heroines inherited houses along with all of the contents. Chris had thought it would be so thrilling to rummage through a strange house and have the thrill of discovering wonderful things in old antique chests and treasures hidden away in dark corners. She had envied these women their ventures. Now she was the heroine, so to speak. And she wondered, feeling a little shiver of excitement, what kind of experiences she would have.

She went into the kitchen and sat down on one of the light gray vinyl chairs framed in silver chrome. In the middle of the table, which matched the chairs, was a small wooden Lazy Susan that held napkins and lamb-shaped salt and pepper shakers: one white, the other black. She noticed that everything in the kitchen looked as if it had come out of a retro catalog featuring the 50's and 60's styles. The counter held a toaster, mixer, can opener, and coffee pot—all were turquoise. Looking down from the refrigerator was a rabbit cookie jar in light pastel colors. The colorful bunny had long ears and a big smile on his face. On a whim, Chris just had to know if there were any cookies in the jar, so she gingerly took it down and sat it on the counter. When she removed the lid, she was amazed to see that the jar was full of chocolate chip cookies that looked homemade. This was a real surprise. She had never thought of Paulette as a person who would make cookies or even have a sweet tooth. She felt a fleeting sadness. She realized she had really never known this woman, this woman who had given her and her children a new life.

Chapter 57

Since school was out for the summer, Chris and her crew of three used every spare moment cleaning, repairing, and painting. They chose from the furniture at the apartment, Paulette's furniture, plus retrieving a few pieces from the attic to initially furnish the house. Chris decided to leave the cleaning of the attic and basement for a later time until they had installed themselves comfortably. They all had such a happy time picking out paint colors and painting that it hardly seemed like real work. Becky picked out a light purple color for her bedroom, while the boys chose a medium blue paint similar to the color of their shared room in Ridgewood, and after much negotiating, the children agreed on a neutral tan for their shared bath.

Chris decided on a lovely cranberry hue for her large bedroom and bath, a color she would have never considered previously. It turned out just gorgeous, and she was so proud of herself for trying something so daring. The kitchen brightened with new creamy yellow walls, and the living and dining rooms, along with the half bath, were refreshed with a clean off-white. In only three weeks, the dreary house was transformed into a delightful home, and they were ready to make the big move.

Chapter 58

Boxes were packed and stacked ready for the move. Mr. Turner and his son Jack were due first thing in the morning, and this time they would move everything. A feeling of tremendous excitement prevailed that evening and to celebrate their last night in the apartment, Chris ordered a large pizza and breadsticks with sauce to be delivered. This had been a very infrequent expenditure these last several months, and Chris felt so generous that she tipped the delivery boy five dollars.

After dinner, the entire family, including Wittles, went across the hall to say goodbye to Mrs. Weber. Thelma was the only person in the apartment complex Chris would miss, and she knew that Thelma would miss them all dearly. She had helped them so much with the care of Wittles, and they would miss her being their weekly dinner guest.

Thelma cried and hugged them all and kissed Wittles' furry face. But Chris couldn't cry. She was too excited about moving out of what Carla had called The Willshire Country Club Estates. Chris promised Thelma that they would visit soon as they said their goodbyes.

That evening, after the kids were asleep, Chris took Wittles down the elevator for her last evening potty. Chris always thought about Carla on these nightly jaunts up and down the elevator, but tonight the thoughts were especially strong. With Carla by her side, the nightly trips didn't seem as scary. It had been three months since Carla's death, and she missed her so much.

Chris opened the door and immediately noticed that one of the lights by the apartment was out. Probably broken by some kids throwing rocks or maybe it had been shot out. Every once in a while there was a noise, like a gunshot at night, that could be heard from her apartment. She felt a little spooked by the semi-darkness but calmed herself knowing this was her last night. Just one more time, one more time to do this by herself tonight. "One more time, one more time" was her mantra now, and she repeated it over and over. Wittles seemed to sense her nervousness. Either the dog was shaking or she was shaking the dog.

The moon was just a curvy slice making the night even darker. The wind blew heavily in spurts, and all kinds of debris rustled around noisily. Wittles finished quickly and they started back to the apartment's door. About 10 feet from the door, three men came around the corner of the building. They were not young, probably around forty or so, and they were laughing as they staggered toward her. Chris automatically felt in her pocket for the little knife she always took with her, but she remembered that she had forgotten it tonight, the first time she had ever done that. She could hear Carla saying, "You dumb ass, you forgot your knife. What did I always tell you?"

In all the months she had lived here, she never had any real confrontations with anyone. She stopped for just a second and then trying to look calm, she continued walking toward the door. One of the men came towards her and stepped sideways blocking her way. He was tall and lean. He wore a sleeveless-type white undershirt, baggy jeans, and a baseball cap worn backwards. Chris was completely intimidated but said, "Excuse me, I need to get by." The man turned around to his buddies and said, "Oh! What have we here, Miss Manners and her little white rat!" His companions laughed menacingly, and this seemed to embolden him. He turned towards Chris then and started to lean down to pick up Wittles. Holding tight to the leash, Chris yanked Wittles out of his grasp and quickly picked her up. The quick action startled Wittles, and she started barking and wiggling to get down but Chris held her tightly in her arms.

One of the other men stumbled toward Chris laughing. "Come on, let me see your little barking rat, lady," and he started to grab for Wittles. Chris was more furious than she was scared, and she stood up as tall as she could and screamed, "Get the fuck out of my way. You touch my dog or me and I will see you in hell." She then used all her strength and pushed past them all and headed quickly to the door. To her surprise, the men just stood there looking dumbfounded. She took advantage of their brief confusion and ran into the building and quickly entered the elevator. Chris' heart was beating wildly, and Wittles continued her frantic barking as the elevator ascended to the fourth floor.

Once inside the apartment, Chris locked and bolted the door. She tried to calm her dog, but Wittles continued her loud barking and started zooming around the rooms. She ran into Becky's bedroom, jumped on the bed, ran over Becky a few times, and then jumped off the bed. She continued to zoom into the other bedrooms, jumping on the beds, and then into the kitchen, running around the kitchen table and then back to the bedrooms. Her behavior woke up all the kids and one by one they came in the living room looking sleepy and confused. Wittles continued her running and barking for several minutes until she exhausted herself. Then she panted heavily and headed for her water dish and drank it dry. After all the commotion, Wittles jumped on Scott's bed and fell asleep.

Chris did not explain the dog's behavior to the kids. They didn't need to know and, hopefully, incidents like tonight would never happen again. She told them that she didn't know what brought on this bizarre behavior and told them to go back to bed, which they did willingly.

Now that everyone was safe, Chris had time to revisit her evening's adventure. She couldn't believe that she had the courage to do what she had done. She had to smile when she remembered her words to the horrid men. She never used the real "f'" word—she always said something like friggin or freakin, or something silly like that. She figured that one of her favorite old TV shows, the Soprano's, had influenced her. They said the "f" word a lot, and it seemed the tough talk worked for them as it had worked for her tonight.

Just as Chris was ready to crawl into bed, the phone rang. She couldn't imagine who would call her at this hour; it was after midnight. She grabbed the phone on the third ring. The caller didn't wait for her to say hello, she just yelled, "Mrs. Cunningham, this is Mrs. Gallagher. I understand that you have a very loud barking dog in your apartment. I had two calls tonight complaining about the noise, and those calls woke me up. Now you know we have been over this before when you first moved in. I told you to get rid of that mutt, but I guess you didn't believe me when I told you NO PETS or OUT. Now get rid of that dog or you will be in violation of your lease, and this time I will be checking—every day if I have to. Do you understand?"

Chris almost laughed. "Mrs. Gallagher, if I decide to keep my dog, does that mean that my lease is broken and I have to leave?"

"Yeah, Princess, that's exactly what it means."

"OK, you old bat, I'll be out tomorrow." Chris hung up the phone and couldn't help laughing out loud. Thank you, thank you, to whoever called Mrs. Gallagher; now she wouldn't have to pay the penalty for leaving before the year's lease was up. Chris fell asleep picturing how Mrs. Gallagher must have looked after she told her she was leaving in the morning.

Chapter 59

Clang! The heavy metal door made such a racket that Lisa jumped. She instantly felt claustrophobic but tried to shake off that feeling. A middle-aged uniformed guard led the way down several dim but orderly corridors and stopped at the double doors that apparently led to the visitor room. The guard unlocked the door and she found herself in a large room with several see-through cubicles. Lisa thought it was just like she had seen on TV and in the movies.

As she nervously glanced around, she saw only two cubicles were in use. Lisa took some deep breaths and tried to calm herself. She was worried because she had no idea how Ted would react to seeing her. It had been over a year since she had thrown Ted out of their apartment and stormed back to New York, out of his life.

After a week of investigating, Lisa found out where Ted was imprisoned. She got permission to visit and drove the one hundred and fifty miles to see him; she was finally here. Ted didn't know she was coming. It would be her surprise.

She had absolutely no clue what she was going to say to Ted, although she had practiced many speeches in the last few weeks. She guessed that everything depended on his reaction. Lisa hoped that Ted would be happy to see her, and hopefully after a year apart he would forgive her for dumping him at a time when he needed her support the most.

It had taken her awhile to admit to herself that she wanted him back in her life. She had been so angry with him for being deceitful, but she realized that she had been pretty deceitful herself.

So here she was, assigned by the guard to one of the little cubicles, sitting and waiting for Ted to come out of the door across from where she sat. Lisa was surprised that there was no glass divider separating them in the cubicle, just a small brown table with a metal chair on either side. She figured that the dividers were for the more violent prisoners. Ted had never been violent, just stupid, and even more stupid to get caught. She reminded herself that what he had done he had done for her, to make her happy. She figured that out months ago when she tired to contact him through his mother. Oh God, his mother, if they did get back together again she would have to face his mother and really apologize for how rude she had been at the end of their telephone conversation.

Lost in her thoughts, Lisa didn't see Ted walking towards her until he was almost to the cubicle. When she did see him, she stood up quickly, her heart racing.

Ted couldn't believe his eyes. Either he was dreaming or Lisa was only a few yards away. He thought that she was more beautiful than he remembered and immediately noticed that she was dressed simply, just jeans and a sweatshirt and she wore almost no make-up.

As Ted arrived at the cubicle, they both stood like mannequins staring at each other for what seemed like forever. Finally Lisa said, "Well, hi." They both laughed as Ted held out his hand and Lisa grasped it tightly.

Lisa was Ted's first visitor since he entered this place eleven months ago, and he didn't know if he could hug her, if he was allowed to hug her, or if she even wanted him to, so he sat down and waited for her to speak. As he waited he wondered why she was here, silently hoping it would be something good.

It was very awkward for both of them, neither knowing what kind of reception would be given by the other. So when Ted started to speak, Lisa held up her hand to stop him. "Let me say this first. I need to say something." She leaned slightly forward toward Ted and let the words flow.

"Well, I want you to know that I feel what you did was wrong and, well, really stupid. But I was wrong and really stupid too when I got so mad and left you the way I did. I've come to regret that and I've missed you, a lot. I know that I have to take some responsibility for being so self-centered and spending your money like crazy. No excuses there. I like to shop. It was fun and you seemed like you could handle it. I wanted to tell you that I'm really sorry, and I wouldn't blame you if you never forgive me, but I think deep down we had something very special going on and I want it back. Now, you can talk." Lisa leaned back against the hard, cold chair and waited for Ted's response.

Ted was flabbergasted, to say the least. He just stared at her for a few seconds, a small grin turning into a large smile. He breathed out a sigh that sounded like "woosh."

"Oh my God, Lisa, you don't know how happy I am to hear you say this. Oh, honey, I've missed you so much, and I thought I'd lost you forever."

Now they were both smiling, big happy smiles and holding each other's hands so tightly that Lisa cried,

"Ow". Ted quickly let go. "Sorry, baby, I wish I could hug or kiss you but don't know if we are allowed. You're the only visitor I've had and—oh hell, why not." Ted and Lisa slowly stood up and leaned across the table, just barely touching each other's lips. Lisa almost fell over the table, and they ended up laughing and feeling like guilty teenagers.

The rest of the hour went by quickly, talking about plans for when Ted was released. Over Ted's objections, Lisa insisted that she would be back to pick him up. "Just tell me the day and time and I'll be here with my bags packed and ready to go. Oh, by the way, where will we be going?"

Ted said he figured the best plan would be to stay in a motel near his mother's house, and he would pick up his meager inheritance from the family lawyer, sell his father's car as soon as they could, and then drive to Florida.

"There's a guy in here who gets out soon. He lives in Florida, and he and I are in the same situation except his family has a lot of connections and we've talked about getting together to see what we can get going. I'll talk to Steven tomorrow and figure out the details. Now that we're going to be together, I'm so excited and now I have a real reason to be enthused about the future." Ted glanced over at Lisa and said, "What do you think? Does Florida sound OK?"

"Well, it sounds great, but is your mother going to just hand over your inheritance?" Lisa got a shiver thinking about facing Ted's mom.

"Oh, I didn't tell you? Mother died. She died of a heart attack a few months ago. Uh, and about the money, she somehow found about you and me and almost disinherited me except for an old car and some money. She left the rest to my kids and Chris."

Lisa looked so surprised, and Ted thought she was confused because he had told her his mother knew about their relationship. "I'm sorry. I did lie to you. I didn't have the nerve to tell Mother about you. She wouldn't have understood. But that bitch I was married to must have let the cat out of the bag, and Mother was so livid she almost completely cut me out of her will. I could have inherited almost half a million dollars, but I guess I'm lucky she even left me $40,000. At least we have that to get a new start."

Lisa gulped. She knew right then that her stupid phone call was the cause of Ted's losing his inheritance, not Chris. She could kick herself. All that money could have made a big difference in their new life together. What a fool she had been. She wished she had kept her temper. Lisa thought for only a second that she should tell Ted the truth, but only for a second. Ted must never know. She would never tell him, afraid of what he might do. Even as she felt guilt, she felt a big relief knowing she wouldn't have to ever face Ted's mother.

Ted mistook Lisa's silence for the fact that he only had $40,000 to his name, and anxiously said, "We will be okay, Lisa. I will do whatever it takes for us to have a good life together," and with a smile added, "legally."

Lisa took Ted's hand and lovingly said, "I know we'll be just fine."

Chapter 60

Chris woke up with a start. She jumped out of bed and was ready to run before she partially awakened and realized she had just come out of a vivid, terrifying dream. Beads of sweat covered her forehead, and she was shaking as she remembered the contents of the dream. Carla was alive and laughing, a laugh that slowly turned into a horrifying scream. Carla's face changed to an almost demonic sight, her skin stretching this way and that, all the while changing colors—mixtures of reds and yellows to purple, then to stark white all the while continuing the horrific scream.

Chris sat down hard on the bed, her head throbbed in pain, and the pain trickled like a waterfall that proceeded to cascade down her face into her neck and finally stopped at her heart where it did a dance in her chest. She tried to breathe regularly, but her foggy brain was still stuck in the dream.

The phone rang and Chris jumped. It rang and rang, but she just sat there and listened to the sound of the ringtone. She had never really listened to the ringtone before; she had just hurried to answer. Now she sat like a statue and just stared at the phone not attempting to answer the call. The ringing finally stopped, and Chris lay back down in her bed. Her body seemed to have settled down, but the dream remained. She thought of Carla, poor Carla, and Chris wondered if Carla had screamed like that before she died.

This was the beginning of many terrifying dreams about Carla. They varied somewhat, but the theme was always the same. Carla laughing, then screaming in terror; Carla's face distorted in some disgusting way. Chris always woke up with her heart pounding and a profound feeling of apprehension. The dreams went on for over a month, and Chris got to the point where she dreaded going to sleep. She wondered if Carla was trying to send her a message of some kind. She really didn't believe in that sort of thing but couldn't think of any other reason why she was having these haunting dreams.

One morning, after one of her Carla dreams, Chris decided she would visit Thelma at the old apartments and maybe go to the cemetery where Carla was buried. She hadn't been to either place for a long time and wondered if it might help her discover why all these frightful dreams were happening.

Chapter 61

The following day, Chris was just awakening from yet another dream. Scotty entered Chris' room and jumped in bed saying, "Happy Birthday, Mom." Do you want me to fix your breakfast and bring it up here? That's what they do on that commercial on TV. The kids make pancakes and cereal and toast and stuff, and it makes the mommy so happy."

Scott's appearance quickly diverted Chris' attention away from her dream, and it slowly disarmed the fear and horror that she had felt just minutes ago. She hugged Scott tightly and gave him a big exaggerated kiss as he giggled and struggled to break free. As if by cue, Bobby and Becky ran to the bed and jumped in with Chris and Scott. All three kids started singing a very sweet but off-key Happy Birthday song, which ended with "you look like a monkey, and you act like one too."

Everyone was laughing and happy. Even Wittles, who jumped up on the bed to join the fun, seemed to have a smile on her furry face.

After she took a nice, long, hot shower, the kids made her a delicious breakfast of frozen waffles toasted in the toaster, Captain Crunch cereal and chocolate milk. Chris had all but forgotten the dream.

The day of her birthday was magnificent. The sun was shining and the sky was cloudless. It was one of those days when the temperature was just perfect for being outside. As a bonus, a gentle breeze was blowing and everyone was in a pleasant mood.

Despite the dreams, Chris realized that she hadn't felt so at ease and contented for a long time. There was a softness about the day, and she felt a somewhat softness about herself. Even though she was a year older, she felt young and secure, a feeling she hadn't experienced in a long, long time. She lifted her face to the sky and thanked the dear Lord that she and her children had gotten safely through the ordeal of the last year and were finally settled in their new home and new life.

Chapter 62

The house was coming along nicely. What a difference soap and water, paint, and decent furniture made. The neighborhood was becoming more familiar with each day, and they had met several very nice neighbors. At this moment, Chris felt at peace with the world.

Laura had called a few days before and invited the family to a cookout in honor of Chris' birthday. With all the commotion of the last few months, they hadn't seen much of the Walkers. The kids were looking forward to being let free in their old neighborhood to see their friends, and Chris was looking forward to just sitting and visiting with Laura and Don again. In the past year, Chris had dreaded going to Ridgewood, dreaded seeing their old house. She had not seen the new family yet, but envisioning them being happy in her house, in her yard, in her pool depressed her. However, that had lost most of its power now since she had her own home and had successfully kept her family intact.

Chris volunteered to make her famous cheese and potato dish that everyone called her "yummy potatoes," and she carried the casserole to the car while the kids grabbed their swimming suits. They were all eager to go, and the conversation was lively the entire ride, the kids chattering away like a bunch of magpies. Today would be fun.

As the car pulled into Laura and Don's driveway, she could see the new family getting ready to leave in their car. The car was a new model Lexus convertible. In the back seat of the candy apple red car were two beautiful blonde girls, probably about Bobby and Scott's ages. A very handsome man was at the wheel, and an attractive blond woman sat next to him. They looked like the perfect little family. Chris' first thought was of envy, but she immediately remembered that everyone thought her family was the perfect family for so long. She reminded herself that nobody really knows what goes on in another person's life. She made herself smile at her children and wondered what they were thinking.

Hurriedly, their old neighbors came out the door to greet them. There were hugs and kisses and lots of excitement. Once settled in the kitchen, Laura poured Chris and herself a glass of wine and soda for all the children. The kids quickly disappeared with Don to the backyard where the grill was heating up.

"I guess you got a good look at the new neighbors. Wish you would have arrived a few minutes later, and they would have been gone." Laura said as she looked at Chris expectantly.

"They sure are a good looking bunch, aren't they?"

"He's nice, she's a bit stuck-up, and the girls are spoiled rotten. I don't want to be mean, but they are not the friendliest people. He speaks to Don when they are both in the yard. I've spoken to him twice since they moved in. I asked her over for a welcome visit one time when they first moved in and she said, 'Thanks, but no thanks. I try not to get familiar with my neighbors—too many problems you know, and we have such a busy social life that there just isn't time. I'm sure you understand.' "

"Chris, I was completely flabbergasted to say the least. I mean I wasn't expecting a relationship like we had, but I felt like I had been, how can I put it, I felt like I had been flicked away like an annoying bug. How can someone be so insensitive?"

Chris didn't know how to answer. On the one hand, she was glad that Laura and the new neighbor weren't the best of friends. But, on the other hand, she could understand how Laura must feel.

"I'm sorry, Laura, but you've still got me." Chris reached over and gave Laura a big hug. "I don't know what I would have done without you all these years, especially this last year, and I feel that it's definitely her big loss not having you for a friend." Laura hugged Chris back, and they let the subject drop and started to enjoy the beautiful day.

The day went by quickly. There was plenty of good food, happy conversations, and enjoying the pool and sun. By late afternoon, everyone was in a pleasant state of relaxation, and it was a hard decision to pack up the kids and go home. Chris gently packed the gifts she was given for her birthday. Laura had given Chris a delicate hand-painted crystal vase filled with bright flowers from her garden, and a framed picture of Laura's family, things Chris would always cherish.

Chris had intended to discuss her Carla dreams with Laura, but she decided not to ruin this perfect day with such a morbid subject. It could wait for another day.

As they were leaving, Don announced, "Laura and I are planning on taking our kids to the lake in a few weeks. We are staying at my parents' cabin for a week. Patty and Jason would really like for Becky, Bobby, and Scott to come along, and of course, you too if you can get off work. What do you think?"

Chris was blown away. "Oh my gosh, that sounds great! I know the kids would love it. I would too. Let me find out if I can get off. Oh my God, that would be so fabulous. Thank you, guys." Chris gave Don and Laura another big hug, and the kids were smiling from ear to ear.

The drive home was as pleasant as the drive there. They were all tired and happy, not to mention that they were all stuffed from all the good food and yummy desserts.

Chapter 63

The next few weeks flew by. Every day seemed better than the last. The whole gang pitched in to clean the attic, basement, and garage. Chris had to work during the week, but in the evenings and on the weekends she spent almost all her free time hard at work.

Although no great treasures were revealed, they did discover an array of useful items that helped make the house more homey. A couple of antique shelves, an old telephone stand, and a rocking chair in need of new paint were unearthed along with some knickknacks and beautiful old linens.

Becky did find an old trunk in the basement that had a wedding dress and veil along with several other items of clothing that looked as if they were from the 20's. A large box of pictures was found in the attic along with old letters and cards. Chris decided to wait until the weather was cooler before she delved into these. Chris also found a smaller trunk that contained many used toys that probably had belonged to Ted. She decided to put them in the old car and offer them to Ted when and if he picked up his car.

Chris gave Paulette's friend, Dora, a beautiful silver tea set and Paulette's pearl necklace. Numerous bags of useable items were donated to the Salvation Army, and many, many garbage bags were put out for the trash.

There was still a lot of work to be done before Chris was satisfied, but the summer was just beginning.

Chapter 64

Ted had always heard the saying about butterflies in the stomach, but until today had never experienced the feeling. Today was the day he would walk out of Talbot prison and be a free man again. A security guard checked off the list of his possessions that he had relinquished the day he first arrived. There wasn't much, just his clothes, shoes, watch, a belt, and his billfold that still contained his driver's license, two credit cards, and twenty-seven dollars. He was also allowed to take a portfolio of papers he had worked on during his stay.

Ted was then escorted to the Warden's office where the Warden gave him the usual spiel about not coming back, checking in with the probation officer, wishing him good luck, and hoping he had learned his lesson, "if you don't want to do the time, don't do the crime." Ted signed a bunch of papers and was given a copy of his release papers. The warden shook his hand and that was that.

Lisa was true to her word and was waiting in the parking lot ready to start her new life with Ted. She had sold all of her household items as well as most of her designer clothing and had only two boxes in the trunk along with her suitcases.

She had been waiting for two hours now and was wondering what was causing the delay. Just as she was getting out of the car to stretch her legs, she saw a security guard walking with Ted toward the gate. Her heart did a flip-flop. This was really going to happen.

When Ted came out of the gate into the parking lot, Lisa ran to him, and they hugged and kissed and laughed like two teenagers. Ted picked Lisa up and twirled her around, her beautiful blond hair flying around her beautiful face. It took them a while until they could settle down, and after all the 'I love yous' and kissing, Lisa got in the driver's seat with Ted next to her. "Well, Mr. Free Man, where to now?"

"You know, honey, I haven't got it all quite figured out, even though I've had plenty of time. I've done nothing but think about this day and dream about today for a long, long time. God knows I've changed my mind a million times." Ted looked over at Lisa and couldn't believe she was actually there. "Gee, baby, you sure look good and smell like a real girl." He pulled her close and kissed her again. This time with such a passion he hadn't felt in over a year.

Lisa smiled and said, "There's a motel about two miles from here. Is that close enough?"

Ted shook his head no. "As good as that sounds, I need to get the hell as far away from here as quickly as possible before they change their minds. Let's drive for a couple of hours and get a place to stay the night. We've waited this long and the farther away from here I'll be able to relax a little. But believe me, as soon as we get there all I want to do is get us naked and make love all night long...or as much as I'm able. You know, it's been so long I may be a virgin again."

Lisa had to laugh. Ted sounded so serious. She didn't say anything, but she hadn't had sex in ages either and felt like she should be able to claim herself a virgin too.

Chapter 65

Chris called Laura and told her the bad news. She hadn't been able to get off work for their week at the cabin. A co-worker had asked off for that week awhile ago, and they would have been short-handed if she left. "Laura, I am so sorry, and the kids are having a fit, but we just can't make it." Laura was quiet for a minute and then said, "Would you be comfortable letting us take your kids? I was hoping that all the kids could play board games or hike or swim and stuff. This may sound selfish, but I was hoping you and I could have some time to ourselves to shop and read and do fun girl things while Don is fishing. Since you can't make it and if your kids don't come, that will mean I'll have to spend lots of time just keeping Jason and Patty occupied. I really need some time alone. But hey, don't worry, if you let us take your three, we'll take good care of the kids. Don likes to spend time with the little darlings, so if he isn't keeping an eye on them I will. What do you think?"

Chris almost jumped with glee! She loved being with her children, but the thought of a whole week by herself was too good to be true. She hadn't been alone for so long, and Laura's idea sounded like heaven. "Laura, I hardly accept. I feel guilty not coming along to help with everything, but your plan would be a win-win situation for both of us. Thank you, dear friend. You are the best. I can't wait to tell my mopey crew that they can go. They have been so miserable ever since I told them I had to work."

"Oh, Chris, I'm the one who feels guilty. You'll be working while we're all on vacation, but I'm so happy that you understand my selfish needs. We'll try to do it again sometime later on in the summer and give you enough time to get off work. Then we can all have a good time. I'm sure Don's folks will let us use the cabin again. They don't go to the cabin as much as they used to."

"Sounds good to me. Just tell me when to have everyone ready."

"Don wants to leave early Saturday morning, probably around seven. Just pack light, but don't forget the bathing suits."

"They'll be ready at seven sharp, and thanks again, Laura."

When they had finished talking, Chris almost ran to tell the kids the change of plans. They were ecstatic. Everybody was happy again. Especially Chris. She thought she probably shouldn't feel quite so excited but put that feeling right out of her mind.

Chapter 66

Saturday came quickly. The sleeping bags and suitcases were all packed. Chris had made cookies and sandwiches for the trip, and she remembered to write a consent letter to give Laura and Don permission to get medical care in case one of her kids had a problem. She couldn't think of anything else, and she started pacing around the kitchen waiting for the car to come. Finally they arrived and with a bunch of hugs and kisses, everyone left.

The only noise Chris heard was Wittles whining. The little dog was confused with all the commotion. Chris grabbed her and sat with her on the sofa, petting away her nervousness until they both started to doze.

Later, Chris got up slowly from the sofa and walked into the kitchen. As she walked, she did a little dance and made up a silly song and sang loudly, "I'm free, I'm free, look at me, can't you see, I'm free. I can have tea, I can climb a tree—oh my, oh me, I'm free." She laughed at herself but kept on singing until the phone rang.

Chris wondered who on earth it could be. She quickly found out that it was Thelma wanting to know when she was planning to visit. "Chris, you said before you would come soon, and I would like to see you. I think I'm scared. Something was printed in the newspaper today about another woman missing around here. It reminded me of our little Carla and that terrible time. Can you please come today? You could maybe make me feel better."

Chris' heart almost stopped. Another woman missing? Could this be connected to Carla's death? Her carefree feeling left abruptly. Chris made the decision immediately. "Uh, sure, Thelma. I have been wanting to come and see you, and I guess today would be a good day. I can't bring the kids though, they're on vacation, but I can come this afternoon and if you like, I'll bring Wittles."

"Oh, would you? I love to see you and my little friend Wittles. Why don't you come, and I will fix a nice sandwich for lunch. You make me very happy to see my nice neighbor again."

So they made plans for lunch. Chris put a dozen or so cookies in a container for dessert and got a bag of chips out of the pantry. The hours went slowly until the time to leave. All the while, Chris was second guessing herself about not telling Detective Spencer Simmons about Vernon and that horrible Terry at the liquor store. Spencer had called a couple of times, even after Carla's case was officially closed and considered an accidental death. Chris didn't encourage his apparent interest. She wasn't ready for any kind of relationship at that time.

She wondered if she should go to the police now. Maybe tell Spencer about the whole thing. She took a couple of extra-strength aspirins for her fast approaching headache and grabbed a piece of paper and wrote down all she could remember about the two guys, Vernon and Terry, who could be suspect. Soon it was time to leave, and Chris and Wittles headed for the car. She sighed rather loudly and mumbled to herself that she would rather be going to the dentist.

Chapter 67

As Chris walked from the parking lot to her old apartment building, she said a silent prayer of thanks that she no longer lived in this depressing place. The rows of dilapidated buildings looked even more sad and demoralizing than she remembered. Crumpled pieces of dirty newspapers, cigarette butts, fast food wrappers, soda and beer cans lay here and there and were crawling along the parking lot pushed by a strong breeze.

Chris tried to escape stepping on a big wad of pink gum. She missed the gum but almost lost her balance as her shoe came down on an unidentified squishy thing, skidding a couple of inches. She held tight to Wittles and managed not to drop her. When she got her footing back, she walked quickly to the entrance and opened the familiar heavy, chipped, and faded black door. She tried to scrape the unknown slime off her shoe by using the steps, hoping to get it all while also hoping not to be able to identify exactly what it was.

The elevator was working, and in a few seconds she was on the fourth floor knocking on Thelma's door.

While she was waiting for the elderly lady to answer, her gaze automatically went to her old apartment door, and then to Carla's door. Many fleeting thoughts roamed around in her head, and she was grateful when she heard Thelma timidly ask, "Who is there, please?"

"It's just me, Chris, and I have Wittles with me."

The door opened quickly, and Thelma greeted them both enthusiastically. She hugged Chris and held out her arms for Wittles, who almost jumped from Chris to the delighted old lady.

The apartment had not changed in the last few months, but she could see a sadness in Thelma. She looked so much older and so tired. She tried to keep a happy facade all through lunch and throughout the visit, but Chris could tell she was not the same.

They had a simple lunch of turkey and cheese sandwiches, chips, Chris' homemade cookies, and the most flavorful brewed coffee Chris had experienced in a long time. While eating, they talked of the new house, kids, Wittles, life at the apartments, and finally got to the point of the visit. They started to discuss the newspaper article.

Thelma put Wittles down and went to get the article from the coffee table and handed it to Chris. "This is the poor girl that has gone away with no one knowing where. She is so pretty and young, and my friend Mrs. Hanson downstairs and me are afraid she is dead—just like Carla."

Chris read the article. The girl's name was Dawn Banks. She lived in one of the apartments in the middle of the complex. She was thirty-two years old with a husband and three children. The article stated that she was last seen three days ago, sometime in the late afternoon or evening. As Chris continued reading the article, she could feel her heart starting to beat faster and faster. She had to sit down and close her eyes and breathe deeply for a short while. Thelma bent over her and patted her on the back. "Chris, I know, I know. Just like Carla. Just gone and I am praying that she is not dead."

Chris finally got control of her emotions and said, "Oh God, Thelma, this can't be happening again. Let's just hope she's found safe soon. It's too terrible to think otherwise."

Then, after a few minutes of further conversation, Chris felt that she should leave. She hugged Thelma, picked up Wittles, and promised to keep in touch. As she left the building, Chris felt such terrible guilt. "What if this was a repeat of Carla's death? What if the police were wrong about the cause of death? If only I had told the police the truth about what I knew…could this be related in some way?"

Chris quickly got in her car and drove to the cemetery. She knew where Carla was buried as she had been there several times before. She found Carla's grave immediately, and she and Wittles sat down in the sparse grass. It was only then that Chris let her emotions go. She cried and cried until she had no more tears. As she talked to Carla's small tombstone, she felt Carla's presence and promised her that she would make things right. She apologized again and again for being so afraid for her family and not telling the police the whole truth. Then Chris just sat there for a long while trying to decide what to do next. Of course, she had to go to the police, but first she wanted to do some investigating on her own. As she started to organize her plan, she could feel the tension leaving her body. She was finally going to do something. She just hoped that if the police had been wrong and Carla had been murdered, and either Vernon or Terry was Carla's killer, she wouldn't be too late.

Leaving the cemetery, she steered the car toward home. Once home, she fed Wittles and changed her clothes. This was done quickly, as she was feeling a real urgency to do something, anything, if it would help find the missing woman. Chris rooted through her junk drawer until she found Spencer's card that he had given her several months ago. She would call him and tell him her fears.

As luck would have it, the dispatcher said that Detective Simmons was not available and put her call to his messages. Chris left him a short message to contact her as soon as possible. She told him it was very urgent.

She then drove toward the restaurant where Carla had worked. She remembered the place was called something like the Steaming Skillet or something similar. She had never been there before but knew it was walking distance from the apartments and on the main road close to the bar that Carla had frequented.

On her second run through that area, she saw a little dinky place called the Blazing Skillet and figured that must be the one. There were several empty parking spaces in front. Chris swiftly pulled into one. She almost ran into the restaurant. Once in the squeaky, green door she looked around the brightly lit interior. The place was deserted except for a lone man standing behind the register. It was only 3:30, in-between the lunch and dinner hours, so no customers were there. That was a good thing. They wouldn't be interrupted.

As she approached the man, she saw that his nametag said 'Vernon, Manager,' and Chris blew out a silent sigh of relief knowing that this was the right place. Deciding to use a direct approach to save time, she asked him, "Did Carla Carbella used to work here?"

Vernon's head snapped up and he stared at her with big brown eyes. He almost shouted, "Hey, who are you, lady, some reporter or police? You know I've told this story a hundred times. Yes, Carla worked here and she was a good worker. No, I know nothing about her death. Now either leave here or I WILL call the police.

The fact that the police had already questioned Vernon came as a shock to Chris. Of course, she thought, there would have been an inquiry at Carla's workplace and an investigation of the people she worked with. It took a second for this to sink in and she replied, "No, I'm not a reporter or anything. Carla was my best friend, and I was curious about you. She told me about your relationship and how she got fired."

"Holy God, don't talk so loud. My wife is in the kitchen, and no, I had nothing to do with her death. How many times do I have to say that?"

"You told her you'd break her neck if she talked to your wife!"

Vernon looked around cautiously and almost whispered, "That was just a stupid comment. I wouldn't hurt a fly. Carla and I were a big mistake. When I told her it was over, she wouldn't let go. My wife was finally pregnant after years of trying and we were so happy. Carla threatened to tell her about us." Vernon stopped for a second and looked toward the kitchen again. "You don't know my wife. Despite the baby and all, she would have left me. Please leave it alone, lady. You know I was here at the restaurant and with my wife at the time Carla died. Believe me the police were all over me, so why are you here digging it all up again?"

"Okay, okay, never mind the reason. I've got to go." Chris quickly left.

Vernon was so stressed out, he put the closed sign on the door and took out a flask from the drawer behind the register and prayed his wife didn't hear any of their conversation.

Chapter 68

Chris felt like she had wasted precious time. Of course, Vernon had been checked out. She would have known if she had only told the police what she knew.

That left Terry. A shudder came over her whole body as she thought of seeing Terry again. It had to be him. Carla had told him some mean and hurtful things the day he grabbed her and tore her blouse coming home from the bar. He probably decided to call in what he thought she owed him. That poor Dawn girl. Was he the one who has her—or had her? Was she still alive?

Chris again felt the immense, immense guilt for telling her lie. As she chastised herself over and over again, she grabbed her cellphone and called Spencer again. When he was still not available, she knew what she had to do.

Chris remembered exactly where Terry's liquor store was located and headed in that direction. As she recalled the last time she was there, she looked up and noticed the sky was getting darker even though it was only a little before five o'clock. She figured it was just what she needed, a dark day to visit that creepy-creep.

When Chris arrived at her destination, she sat deciding what she was going to do once she was in the liquor store. She was afraid to be direct with Terry as she had been with Vernon. She couldn't think of any real plan and decided to just wing it. So gathering all her courage, Chris started out of the car. Remembering again that dark spooky store, she sat back down quickly. She grabbed the phone and called Spencer a third time. When the dispatcher told her Detective Simmons was not available again, she left a message with the dispatcher telling her who she was and to please have Detective Simmons call as soon as possible.

By now it was even darker and had started raining in torrents. Chris felt like she couldn't have scripted a better scenario than this one for what she had to do. Somehow Snoopy came to mind, sitting on his doghouse typing, "It was a dark and stormy night." She even laughed a little to relieve her tension.

"Okay, I'll just go in and buy some wine and check things out." This time she did make it out of the car and walked quickly to the liquor store's door. She had no umbrella and her hair and clothes were soaked.

The store's lighting was between dim and gloomy. She figured Terry did this on purpose to hide the store's appalling lack of cleanliness and the dust-laden merchandise.

As Chris' eyes adjusted to the light, she saw Mr. Creepo in all his glory sitting behind the cluttered counter. Chris tried to calm her queasiness as she pretended to check out the wine selection. It was hard not to notice that Terry wasn't his obnoxious self as he was the last time she was here. He didn't speak a word to her and was fidgeting with something while a cigarette hung from his mouth.

Chris tried to nonchalantly look around, noticing the layout of the store. She saw two doors and wondered where they led. But she figured this was of no importance since she really needed to find out where Terry lived and have the police check it out.

She picked out a medium-priced Chablis and walked to the counter. Terry was standing perfectly still and was looking down at something very intently. When Chris got to the counter, Terry's eyes shot up and he just stared at Chris. She felt like she had been hit by a lightning bolt and took a step backwards. Still staring, he took her money without saying a word and handed her the change.

At this point, Chris decided she definitely wasn't the Nancy Drew type and left as quickly as her feet would take her. If she had eyes in the back of her head, she would have seen Terry smiling.

Pouring rain hit her in the face and drenched her again as she headed for the car. She fumbled through her purse for the car keys and got in and locked the doors. She shook uncontrollably not knowing if it was from the coolness of the rain or the horror that was Terry. She felt there was an evil presence in him and remembered that she had the same terrifying feeling the first time she had seen him. Evil, just evil.

Still shaking, she checked her cell phone and couldn't believe Spence still had not answered. So she figured she would wait until Terry left the liquor store and follow him home. Then she would talk to any police officer she could reach and have them deal with Terry. At this point, Chris was almost positive he was the right man. If she was wrong, she was wrong. At least she could tell herself she tried to right her wrongdoing.

Chapter 69

Chris moved her car across the street, tucking it in between a black truck and a dark-colored van. Here she would have a good view of the liquor store; the darkness and rain were a real asset now. The hours of business were posted on the door. The store should close at 7:00 today. If Terry did close at 7:00, she would only have to wait a little over an hour, so she grabbed an old green jacket from the back seat and tried to dry herself and then put the jacket on to help warm her. Her hair was a mess and her clothes wet and wrinkled. Although this was not the time to worry about her appearance, she certainly hadn't planned to look like a drowned rat when and if she saw Spencer.

Chris finally admitted to herself that she had some kind of feeling for Spencer. Even though they had only been together for official business relating to Carla, she now felt something could definitely be there. Maybe a good friend. Chris hoped that Spencer felt something too. She really didn't know if he had a girlfriend or was serious about someone. She didn't even know if he was married, although she had noticed the lack of a ring.

Chris quickly forgot Spencer when she saw a light come on in an upstairs room in the liquor store. So, one of the doors led to the second floor. How had she not remembered the building had a second floor? The light stayed on a full fifteen minutes or so and then darkness.

She wondered what was upstairs, possibly storage, or an office, or a bathroom. The place had to have a bathroom. Another five minutes went by, and Chris was staring at the front door expecting Terry to be leaving at any time. While she was so absorbed watching the door, her eye caught another light go on, this time in the basement. The light was an eerie gray-blue color. So now it was clear the two doors were for steps upstairs and down to the basement. Maybe the basement was the storage room. "Ha! Elementary, my dear Watson." She was getting the hang of this detective stuff.

Again, the light was switched off after a short time, and then the whole building was in darkness. Terry came out and went directly to the side of the building and got into his dilapidated car.

Oh, here goes, Chris thought. She waited until he was further down the street and started following him. He didn't drive very far, just past the apartment complex a few blocks to the Pioneer Bar. Carla's bar.

"What the heck," Chris almost yelled, "you stupid idiot. Now what are you doing? How long are you going to sit on your sorry butt at a bar and booze it up. Go home you, dumb ass. I've got to pee, and I can't spend all night waiting for you to go home."

Chris really did have to find a restroom soon. What a predicament! Then, almost out of the blue, a thought crossed her mind. It made sense. Wasn't Terry walking towards the apartments the night he and Carla fought? Maybe he was walking in that direction because the liquor store WAS his home. He could live upstairs and maybe that eerie-lighted basement was where he took Carla. Maybe when Carla was in the store he somehow got her to go down there, or maybe she was overpowered and forced to the basement. Maybe Dawn is now in that basement. Maybe she is still alive—maybe,

maybe, maybe, all kinds of maybes went flitting around in Chris' mind.

With this new and exciting theory, Chris felt like she would be wasting time waiting for Terry to leave the bar. She wished now he would drink himself silly and give her time to figure this whole thing out.

She found an open gas station and made a quick stop. Then she drove back to the liquor store. The rain had reduced itself to a drizzle when Chris parked her car at the same place where she waited earlier. She hoped Terry would be at the bar for a while as she was determined to look closer at the windows.

Chris was calm as she removed a flashlight from the emergency kit in the trunk and then crossed the street. Trying to avoid all the big puddles, she hurried to the back of the building. There she saw a fire escape ladder to the second floor. The last rung of the ladder was way over her head and definitely beyond her reach. She looked around for a fallen branch or some kind of pole or anything long, but could see nothing that would help. "Just my luck, that would have been too easy."

Next step was to check the windows. She walked around the building in the wet, muddy grass and checked all of the first floor and basement windows. They were all locked tight. Every window had some sort of curtain or covering, so she could not see in.

A passing car's headlights shined on Chris just as she finished checking the last window near the front door. She crouched down behind a bushy shrub and held her breath. The car thankfully passed by, and as she went to get up she noticed a basement window she had obviously missed. It was hidden behind the shrub. She pointed her flashlight towards the window and could see a big horizontal crack going completely across with smaller cracks splintering out from it. Without thinking, she gave the end of the flashlight a hard push against the window and most of the glass fell inward, making a tinkling sound as it hit the floor.

This impulsive action made Chris stop and think. "What am I doing? Breaking and entering, I could go to jail. My kids would have two jailbirds for parents." She gave a nervous laugh at the thought of Ted and her behind bars together, but the thought ended abruptly when she heard a muffled sound coming from the basement.

Chris carefully put her hand through the ragged glass and pushed aside the material used as a curtain. Looking around, the beam of the flashlight showed a large room with lots of shelves and boxes. The floor was littered with papers and what looked like trash. She saw a blur of something scurrying by, maybe rats, hopefully cats. She moved the light toward the sound and saw something that could be a person sitting in the corner. Squinting, Chris saw it was a person now mumbling loudly and wiggling around. Oh my God, she found her. Now what to do?

"Hey, in there, it's okay. I'm not Terry. I'm calling the police now. Just hang on."

Chris reached in her pocket for the phone to call 911 and found nothing there. She checked the other pocket, same thing. "Oh no, where is that damn phone? It must have dropped out somewhere around the house. What do I do now? Where is Spence?" She had to find her phone, but finding it in this dark, watery mess could take forever and she didn't have forever.

Close to panic, Chris remembered the old rotary phone sitting on Terry's counter when she had purchased the wine hours before. She would have rather done anything, ANYTHING else than go into that basement, but what other choice did she have. She had to get to a phone.

Chris mentally measured the window and figured she could just fit. She fumbled for the latch through the shattered glass and found the handle and pulled it up. The window opened inside and she looked down to see some stacked boxes. Not knowing how stable the boxes were, she gingerly lowered herself in the window, being very mindful of the broken glass below. The boxes held her weight and she sighed a thankful sigh.

Once on the floor, she shined her flashlight toward the girl and walked precariously to the corner where the trembling girl sat. Chris tried to ease the tape carefully from her mouth, but could see it was causing her pain, so she ripped it off with one swift pull.

The girl yelped and gasped the air. "Thank you, thank you! Get me out of here, please get me out of here before he comes back. You don't know. He's crazy, he's evil. Untie me, please, and let's get out of here. Hurry, hurry, let's go."

"Hey, calm down now. I've got to get to a phone to call the police for help and find something sharp to cut your ropes. I'm going upstairs, but I promise to be right back. Just a couple more minutes, all right?"

"No, no, don't leave me. You don't know, he's nuts. Oh God, please hurry, hurry!"

Chris could barely see the stairs and followed the now dimming beam of her flashlight up to the basement door. Thank the dear Lord, the door wasn't locked. She hurried to the counter and easily found the antiquated phone. She was so relieved. She lifted the receiver and waited for a dial tone but there was no sound. Chris panicked. "No, no, no, this can't be," she cried as she grabbed the cord and followed it under the counter just to find there was no plug at the end, just a smooth cord. She scattered the contents of the desk, feeling for a cell phone. No cell phone.

Chris' mind was racing, "What to do now? Got to get out of here." She looked around for something sharp to cut Dawn's ropes. Fumbling frantically around, she found what she thought was a box-cutter on top of some boxes behind the counter and hurried to the basement door to free Dawn.

With the cutter in one hand and the failing flashlight in the other, Chris cautiously descended the basement steps, all the while wondering if she should just leave and get help. But Dawn's pitiful cries urged Chris on to free her and make a quick getaway.

The cord used to tie Dawn was very thick, and Chris had to be careful not to cut skin along with the cord. The process was very slow, but she managed to free Dawn's arms and was starting on her ankles. They were both startled when the sound of a car and then a car door slam was heard from the broken window.

Chris immediately turned off the flashlight. Dawn grabbed at Chris, "No, no we've got to get out of here. Do my ankles."

Chris pulled away. She couldn't see a thing. "Be quiet, maybe he didn't see the light. Put your hands behind your back like you are still tied and I'll think of something. Come on, Dawn, just please shut up."

Dawn continued whimpering. Then, sure enough, the front door opened with a loud squeak, and a light came on upstairs. Chris clutched the box-cutter tightly in her hand. It was the only weapon she had, but she didn't know what to do with it. Her mind racing, she thought she might catch him by surprise when he came down the steps and cut his legs, or hide the cutter under her jacket and then threaten him with it. She gripped the weapon more tightly.

Both she and Dawn were trembling now. Chris kept whispering for Dawn to keep quiet when she remembered she had pulled the tape off Dawn's mouth. Terry would surely know when he saw that. Then she abruptly remembered she had left the basement door open. She knew then, there would be no surprises.

They heard movement from above and heavy footsteps walking around.

Dawn whispered, "Hide, hide, then stop him. Please stop him. Oh my dear Lord, help us."

The basement was so dark and Chris wasn't sure where to hide. She stumbled toward the broken window, her footsteps crunching the glass. The window did let in a very dim glow, and she could barely see the silhouette of boxes. As she groped desperately at them to find somewhere to hide, the basement light clicked on, and the whole room was illuminated.

As Terry started down the steps, he could see Chris clearly. He smiled menacingly and slowly his left hand came out of his pocket pointing a small gun directly at her. "What do we have here? Ah, it's you. I remember you. You were here a while ago. You were acting kinda nervous and weird. You sneaky little bitch, who are you? You know, I could shoot you right here and now and get away with it. Breaking and entering is a serious crime." He laughed as his eyes shifted to Dawn, "Well, I guess I won't do that. Wouldn't want the cops nosing around here, would we?" He laughed again at his little joke, and then his attention focused on the window. "What the hell did you do to my window? Look at it. You broke it and there's glass all over and rain coming in. So who are you anyway, and what do you think you're doing here? Answer me, lady in the green coat. Why are you messing with my life?"

Chris couldn't say a word. She stood petrified and just starred at Terry who was now so agitated that he seemed to be talking to himself.

Terry sat down on the bottom step still aiming the gun at Chris. He started mumbling, "Two of them, what do I do, what do I do now? Damn it, you've ruined everything." His right leg was visually jumping nervously up and down, making a thumping sound.

Still pointing the gun, Terry's stared at Dawn with such menace that she immediately started whimpering, her body trembling, her eyes as round as oranges. "You got the tape off, huh? So what did you tell this law-breaking piece of crap? Answer me, you little slut, answer me or I'll..."

His voice trailed off as he got up and walked toward Dawn who instinctively held her arms up to shield her face. Terry swore again as he realized that her arms had been untied. He checked her legs to see if they were secure and then turned quickly to Chris. She had not moved. She felt glued to the floor.

Terry slowly walked to where Chris stood. His cold, blank eyes terrified her. "Drop the cutter. Drop it right now or I'll shoot you and you know I'll do it."

Chris did as she was told. Terry bent down to pick it up and as he was rising, he swung his hand that held the gun and hit Chris smack on the chin. Chris fell back but caught herself with her hands to soften the fall. The broken glass on the floor cut into her hands. Dawn screamed and Terry turned to her, "Shut up or I'll shut you up. Now where's the fucking tape? You know, two of you is just one too many."

Terry looked around and said, "Aw, damn, it's upstairs. Listen, ladies, no one moves. If you move one inch, I'll shoot you. Do you hear, I'll shoot you."

Terry ran up the stairs and in a matter of seconds was back with the tape and more rope. "Well looks like no one moved, smart choice."

"Get up, green coat lady, and sit over here next to your friend."

Chris painfully got up and picked some glass out of her hands as she walked to where Dawn was sitting. Her hands were bleeding and painful. Terry grabbed her shoulders and roughly pushed her down and she sat down with a plop close to Dawn. He tied her hands behind her and then tied her legs. Chris seemed to still be in a daze. She couldn't comprehend that this was really happening to her. Things like this happened on TV or in the movies, but not in real life, not in her life.

Terry turned to Dawn and quickly tied her wrists. She was shaking with fear and trying to gulp back her sobs. After both women were secured, Terry seemed to relax a bit but continued to talk to himself. "Gotta fix that window, damn it, more work to do. Gotta clean up the glass. Don't want my cats to get out or cut their feet. Got to decide what to do now. Everything is so messed up. Feed the cats, get water, but no, first the glass. The window, it's broken, gotta fix the window."

Terry continued to mumble as he swept the glass and put heavy layers of duct tape over the window.

While Terry was taping the window, Chris looked

around the basement and for the first time could see it clearly since the light was on. It was a large room with many wine and liquor boxes stacked along the wall under the window, the wall directly opposite where she and Dawn were sitting. She couldn't tell if the boxes were full or empty, but they were stacked four or five high.

To the left of the stairs was a cement wall with a small doorlike enclosure. It looked like someone had just knocked part of the wall down to make the entrance. The door was just large enough for a person to squeeze through. Chris shuddered as she wondered what was on the other side.

The rest of the room was cluttered with newspaper and old plastic storage containers, the contents spilling over the tops with stuff that looked like plain junk: a ball-cap, ice cube trays, rags, dirty clothes, just junk.

As her eyes followed the walls around the room, they stopped abruptly at the corner across from where she and Dawn sat. Chris let out a low, almost mournful cry. There on a large nail hung Carla's brown coat and just below it on the floor was her tapestry purse.

The sight of her dead friend's possessions seemed to nudge her to reality, and she finally realized what a predicament they were in.

Terry was on the move again, going up the stairs mumbling something about cats, and Chris took this time to talk to Dawn, who was still trembling and crying softly.

Dawn looked like she was in shock. Her big brown eyes had tears in the corners just waiting to fall. She had beautiful black hair and her skin was a coffee with two creams color. She was a small, slim, beautiful woman.

"Dawn, look at me. Tell me what the heck has been going on here. How long have you been down here? Has he—uh—hurt you? How did you get here?"

Dawn spoke in a whisper. "I think I've been here a long time, maybe two or three days. He hasn't touched me yet except to push me around and always yelling that I'm a whore and that I've been leading him on. I guess I was a little because he kept talking about me paying him back some day, you know, when he let me take wine and things without paying for them."

"How did he get you down here anyway?"

"Well, the other day he said one of his cats had a litter of six kittens down in the basement, and he wanted me to see them, that they were so cute and all. I was dumb enough to believe him, and when I got down here, he pushed me down and put that gun to my head and told me not to move. I was so scared that I let him tie me up. This has been such hell. He wouldn't even let me up for a long time, what seemed like a day. Finally, after I wet myself a few times and was starving he took me upstairs to wash myself and gave me something to eat and drink. This morning he said we were going to have a candlelight dinner, and he was going to give me a bath and we'd have some fun.

"And oh, he has cats, lots and lots of cats. We've got to get out of here because I don't think I can take another night of those cats. I think they live in that creepy little room over there, and when he shuts off the lights it's so dark, but the cats come around meowing and rubbing themselves up against me. They are so filthy and smelly and have fleas that jump on me, and the fleas bite. Look, my legs and ankles are full of flea bites. And I can't brush them off because my hands are tied. I can't scratch and they itch so bad. Maybe they won't bite you so much since you have long pants and sneakers, but, me with shorts and flip-flops, I give them a lot of skin to bite. I kept thinking the cats would bite me too, but they just rub and sometimes lick. It's so disgusting. Oh my God, I wonder if he's still planning the dinner and bath and stuff. Maybe since you're here he'll leave me alone. But the cats, they must kill mice or something because every once in a while you hear them running, and they, or something else, make horrible noises. I think they must kill rats or maybe each other—oh no, here he comes."

Dawn quickly stopped talking as Terry came down the steps with two large pans, one with water and one with cat food. It wasn't but a few seconds and a dozen or more cats came running out of the strange door towards Terry. They were the dirtiest, ugliest, mangiest cats Chris had ever seen. She was sure no cat brush had ever touched their fur.

"Come here, my sweet little furry kittens. Come see what daddy has today. Hello there, Ruffles and Bozo. Oh there you are Princess with your babies. Don't fight now, there's plenty for all of you."

Terry looked up at Dawn and Chris, "These are my babies, aren't they all so beautiful?"

Dawn said sarcastically, "Yes, they are lovely."

Chris ignored the question. She swallowed hard and gathered her courage and said, "Looks to me like Carla's purse and coat over there. Did you kill her?"

Terry quickly walked over to Chris, "What did you say? Did you know that sneaky little tease?"

"Well, did you kill her?"

"Hell no, I didn't kill her; Carla killed herself. Running into that storm without her coat or anything. She came in here freezing cold. She said she was so sorry for being mean to me the other day. I knew she was lying so I thought I'd have me some fun. I just laughed and gave her some wine to warm up. She was very thankful. After quite a few drinks, I told her about the kittens in the basement. Something about women and kittens, they both fell for it."

Terry looked at Chris. "Hey, lady, don't look at me like that. I didn't have a chance with her. She was a wildcat."

"We were getting nice and warm, and Carla was getting drunk. I started pulling her upstairs to have some fun, when she kicked me where it hurts and ran out the door. After I could walk, I was going to follow her but couldn't see a damn thing, the snow was so heavy and blowing like a bitch. Anyway, I never saw her after that and I heard they found her frozen like a popsicle. Ha! I figure she got what she deserved. So shut up, you hear, you trouble maker."

"How can you talk about her like that? You must be sick. Oh, poor Carla."

Without saying another word, Terry got the tape and quickly taped both their mouths. "That should shut you two up for a while. I got to think what to do, and I don't need all your quacking."

Terry turned then, looked around the room, went up the stairs, and clicked off the lights. Darkness rapidly consumed the room. It was completely black.

Panic hit Chris seconds afterward. She struggled against her bonds until she was weary and breathing heavily through her nose.

The cats came shortly after with their happy mewing and rubbing, being glad that they had company for the night. Chris could hear Dawn's pathetic moaning, reminding her about the fleas. She was very thankful that she had on jeans and gym shoes and her legs and feet were covered.

Time passed, Chris didn't know how long. All she could do was sit and think and listen. The cats had left, leaving an incredible stench. The only sounds were indistinguishable coming from the cavelike room. She thought and thought of a way to get out of this horrible situation, and then after a while when she was thoroughly and mentally exhausted, she fell into a restless, disturbed sleep.

Chapter 70

Chris awakened with a start. In the din of the basement, she could see a cat had jumped on her lap and was licking her nose. She winced and jerked her head to the side making the cat jump to the floor. The stinky cat shortly lost interest and moved out of her sight.

The basement wasn't pitch black now. There was a dim light showing under the broken window. Terry must have missed a spot when he taped it the night before. As her eyes adjusted, Chris could see that Dawn was awake. The two women looked into each other's eyes for a while, not able to communicate any other way. Chris saw that Dawn looked hopeless, her eyes full of despair.

Reality hit with a bolt, and Chris again struggled to get free. After several minutes, she stopped abruptly when she heard a noise. Dawn had heard the sound too. It was coming from the broken window and was plainly a song from ABBA, The Dancing Queen, the tune Chris had programmed in her cell phone.

It took only a second to put two and two together. The cell phone was ringing. How could that be? Yes, her cell phone was definitely ringing. It must have fallen out of her pocket while she was crouching behind the bush. She had apparently overlooked it when she had searched for it in the darkness of the night and the rain.

She chastised herself for not looking longer. All of

this could have been avoided. But she put those thoughts aside and was just thankful that it was working. She now had some hope; maybe it was Spencer calling her back. Had it rung during the night while she was sleeping? She didn't know but she had to get to that phone before Terry came down. Chris figured it must be early dawn and hoped that Terry wasn't an early riser.

Now, both she and Dawn started laboring to get free. Chris found that she could scoot on her bottom and push a little with her hands. However, when she did her hands painfully reminded her of the cuts from the glass the night before.

Regardless of the pain, she had to find a way to get to the phone. She thought about the broken glass. Maybe Terry hadn't swept it all. She scooted in the direction where the glass had fallen. It seemed to take forever. Then she felt around the floor for any shards, but Terry had done a thorough job, and not a piece was found.

Chris' mind was going twenty miles and hour. She desperately needed something sharp enough to cut the rope. She remembered Terry had taken the box-cutter upstairs and couldn't remember seeing anything in the basement that would do the job.

The phone rang again, taunting her. Just a few feet above, but no way to get to it. Chris could feel the tears of hopelessness starting, but she just couldn't give in. Who knew what Terry was capable of doing? He was obviously a sociopath. Who knew what he had done in the past. Maybe he was a murderer.

As she was thinking, thinking so hard, she swore she heard a voice in her head saying, "Come on, princess, use your punkin' head. What did we use for protection all those nights when we took the dogs out? You are such a wimp. Get with it!"

Chris didn't believe in all that mystical stuff but knew that's how Carla would talk to her if she were here. The knives, those puny little knives that probably wouldn't have done any good in a bad situation, but did give them a sense of some security while they were walking the dogs outside the apartments.

Carla's purse, of course! She kept her little knife in the lining of her purse. If Terry checked her purse, he probably wouldn't have found it. Chris prayed as she scooted to the corner where Carla's purse lay. The pain in her hands was forgotten, substituted by hope and anticipating getting to the phone.

Thank God the purse was on the floor. With great difficulty, she managed to manipulate the opening and felt around for the torn lining. Sure enough, there was the little pocketknife hidden in the bottom. Chris silently thanked Carla and then scooted as fast as she could over to Dawn.

Chris' hands were throbbing now, but she got the knife open. Once Dawn saw the knife, she muffled some sounds of joy and turned her back to Chris and raised her arms as far as they would go. The little knife was sharper than she had imagined, but cutting through the rope was slow. Chris knew she must have nicked Dawn a couple of times because Dawn had winced, but finally her arms were free.

Dawn ripped off the tape from both their mouths and immediately cut through the ropes on her own legs and then cut Chris free. Once both were free, they hugged each other tightly, and Dawn started to talk. Chris whispered, "Shh, he might hear us. Stay put, don't make a sound while I get the phone." Dawn nodded in agreement and sat down scratching her legs.

Everything hurt as Chris quietly walked to the

window. She carefully climbed up onto two boxes to reach the window. She removed the tape from the bottom of the window to give her enough space for her arm to reach the phone. It was lighter outside now and she found it quickly. There it was, resting in the little shrub outside the window. The shrub must have protected it from being ruined by the rain. She grabbed it and quickly dialed 911. She spoke quietly to the operator and rapidly told him where they were and what had happened. Chris asked that Detective Spencer Simmons be notified.

The operator told her to stay on the line, and he asked her questions and tried to calm her until the police arrived.

Dawn got up gingerly and walked toward Chris. "Maybe we could climb out the window while we can."

The 911 operator heard Dawn and told Chris that the police were only a few minutes away, and they should stay quiet. The noise might alert Terry. As promised, in minutes they heard a commotion at the front door. Terry came flying down the basement stairs with his gun drawn. He registered shock that they were untied but swiftly grabbed Dawn by her hair and pulled her and pushed Chris into the cavelike door. "You two, don't make a sound or I'll shoot the first cop that hears you. I've got nothing to lose now, so you'd better listen to me and shut up or someone's going to die."

Terry's hand was shaking hard, and he had a manic look on his face that scared the heck out of both women.

Once the women were in the cave, Terry started stacking liquor boxes in front of the opening. It didn't take long before it was so dark they couldn't see a thing. The ground they stood on felt like an oozy mud. The smell was overpowering and several cats ran over to them excited and confused. Chris could hear sounds but couldn't make out words. Both women trembling and almost sick with the damp and smelly enclosure were horrified that they were still under Terry's crazy control.

Soon it was quiet and then they heard Terry taking the boxes away. "Well, you saved a couple of lives by being quiet. I could have easily shot two or three of them in a flash. Those stupid cops, I guess I showed them who's smarter. They're all gone now. Couldn't find a thing out of place. Ha! What a bunch of idiots."

Terry was again moving his gun back and forth between the women, his hands still shaking as he was very agitated now. "How in the hell did you get the ropes off, and why did the cops come here in the first place? What did you...?" He stopped in mid-sentence when Chris' cell phone started ringing. "What the hell," Terry shrieked. He started walking toward the sound.

Chris remembered dropping the phone when Terry came charging down the steps. "Where did this come from?" He was sure he had searched Chris before he tied her up.

Terry grabbed the phone, threw it to the floor, and stomped on it. It smashed in several pieces. "Who are you, Houdini or something? Where did you get the goddamned phone? I'm asking you a question, Houdini. Where did you get the phone?"

Neither Chris nor Dawn answered. "Get over there, you two, while I get the tape, no shenanigans or you know what will happen."

Terry's face was a mask of sweat, and the gun was waving as he mounted the steps.

Dawn was crying now. "What happened, why did

they leave us here, Chris? We should have gone out the window when we had the chance."

A loud thump came from upstairs. Suddenly, people were talking, and then, like an angel sent from God, a young policeman came down the stairs. "It's okay, ladies, we got the guy. You are safe now."

Chris and Dawn ran to the policeman and hugged him. "What happened up there? We thought you left us."

"Well, we knew you two ladies were in here somewhere, so everyone made a big pretense of leaving, except me. I hid behind one of the shelves and waited for him to show us where you both were. The other officers drove off and parked a little away and waited for me to contact them. When the guy came upstairs. I was going to taze him, but I saw he had a gun so I sneaked up behind him and hit him pretty hard. He's out cold. An ambulance is on the way for him, and I need to determine if either of you need an ambulance, or can you ride to the hospital in a squad car?"

Both said they were fine and didn't need to go to the hospital, but the officer insisted that it was police procedure for them to be checked out.

Chris said, "I just really need to go to the bathroom," and Dawn nodded her head in agreement.

The ambulance came and Terry was taken away. Chris and Dawn were driven to the hospital and Dawn's family was notified. Chris said her family was out of town, and she didn't need to call anyone.

After a thorough examination, Chris' hands were washed and bandaged and she was pronounced healthy. Dawn was given a painkiller and salve for her legs, and both women got a tetanus shot. They were then taken to the police station and told the detectives what had happened and answered many questions. Finally, they were allowed to go home.

Dawn's husband and three daughters were there to take her home, and they were all so happy. Chris was glad for Dawn but wished she had someone there to be happy with. She did not want to tell Don and Laura and certainly not the kids. She would wait until they come home and maybe tell Laura then.

Chris gave Dawn a big hug, and they both held on tight. They exchanged phone numbers and both said they would call soon. They had been through so much together that they felt like friends. A policewoman told Chris that she would take her home and her car would be delivered to her soon.

Chapter 71

Once home, the policewoman asked if she should stay with Chris for a while. Chris told her that she would be fine and didn't need her to stay. As the woman was walking away, Chris remembered, "Oh, there are a dozen or so cats in that basement that need care. They aren't bad cats, just very dirty and probably hungry." The policewoman nodded and said she would report that.

It was only then that Chris remembered Wittles. The poor little thing had been alone almost twenty-four hours with no food or being let outside. Chris hurried inside and called for her, but she didn't come running. Chris quickly spotted Wittles under the kitchen table and she was whining. By the back door was a big puddle, and Wittles thought she was in trouble.

Chris reached down and picked up her furry baby and told her over and over how sorry she was. She petted her and asked her to please forgive her, and when they had both calmed down, she let her outside and proceeded to fill her empty food and water dishes.

Chris took a long shower and washed her hair three times. She needed to get the stink and dirt off her immediately. Letting her wet hair hang, she put on her old robe and slippers, poured a bowl of Cheerios, and fixed some hot tea.

While she was eating, the phone rang and it was

Laura. "Where have you been? I've been calling you since we got here yesterday. We've been so worried. We tried to call your house phone and cell phone a few times early this morning, and I told Don we were going to come back home if you didn't answer this time.

"Oh, Laura, I'm so sorry. I've been having problems with my home phone and have no idea where my cell phone is," Chris lied. "Don't worry about me, and the phone here at home is okay now. I hope you're all having a good time. I'm great really, just enjoying some time by myself."

"Well, I'm so relieved. I do miss you, but this place is amazing. The lake, walking trails, caves, we hope to do it all. Don's father has this little fishing boat and fishing stuff. The weather is perfect and the kids are swimming with Don right now, so I'll call you back sometime later so they can talk to you."

"Hey, that's great! Sorry I worried you. Go read a book. Ha ha."

"Actually, I'm in the middle of *Life of Pi*. It's awesome. I'll give it to you when we get back. You'll like it. Okay, Chris, talk to you soon. Love ya."

"Love ya too. Bye now."

Chris finished her meal and spent the next part of an hour holding Wittles and telling her what she had been through. She finally let loose with the tears and cried and cried. Wittles looked at her with big understanding eyes and tried to lick away the tears. This made Chris cry all the more.

As darkness came on, so did the rain. The rain poured and was joined by lightning and thunder.

Even though thunder was booming and lightning lit

the sky, Chris found it very soothing to be home, dry and warm and not afraid, so glad not to be in Terry's basement. They slept. It was one of those times when you go in and out of sleep and are so relaxed you never want to move, a peaceful sleep.

Wittles and Chris must have slept for several hours when she was abruptly awakened by a bell. It took her a moment to clear her foggy brain before she realized that the noise was the doorbell. Funny, no one had rung the doorbell since they had moved here and the sound was unfamiliar to her.

She leaped off the sofa, accidentally pushing Wittles off her lap. Wittles ran towards the door barking ferociously. Chris' first thought was of Terry, but she put that quickly aside. He was in jail or somewhere where she prayed he was locked in tight.

There was no peephole in the door so she couldn't see who was there. Chris grabbed Wittles and cautiously moved the living room curtain back a bit. The porch light wasn't on so she only saw a dark figure in the shadows. The bell rang again. Wittles started barking again. Chris' heart raced.

Just then her home phone rang. She answered it quickly and with a low voice. "Hello."

"Chris, this is Spence. I'm on your front porch. Sorry to be here so late but could you let me in? I really need to talk to you."

"Uh, yes, of course. Hold on, I'm right here."

Relieved, Chris let Spence in. Wittles barked at the strange man, but when Spence knelt down to pet her, she amazingly quieted right down and licked his hand.

"Some watchdog you have here, Chris," Spence said with a smile.

"Yeah, she's not very big but can be quite noisy."

Spence signaled toward the sofa, "Let's sit down. You look exhausted."

Chris realized she must look a mess. She hadn't done anything to her wet hair, and it had dried in tangles. With no make-up, hair looking like a wild woman, and wearing her old bathrobe and slippers, she was really embarrassed. "Oh my gosh, I must look terrible. We've been sleeping almost all day."

"You look just fine. After what you've been through, you look great."

Chris tried to comb her hair with her fingers, but it was no use.

Spence started slowly, "I am so sorry that I wasn't available to help you, Chris. I feel like a jerk. But let me tell you what happened. My partner and I were on a stakeout all day Thursday and Friday. When I finally got home late Saturday morning, I was so wiped out I just went to bed. I woke up on and off, and it was so dark and rainy I just kept sleeping until early Sunday morning. As luck would have it, I left my cell phone in the car. I always keep my phone near me, but the one day," Spence stopped and swallowed hard. "The one day I didn't had to be when I was really needed. And, uh, anyway, by the time I got your messages, I tried to call your cell, but got no answer. I called a few more times, nothing."

Spence continued. "Saturday and today were my days off, but I called in a while ago to check on something, and my boss informed me they found the woman who was kidnapped. When he mentioned your name, I realized that you were calling me for assistance. I can't tell you how I feel, knowing you were in such peril and I was sleeping away. Do you want to talk about it? I'm here now and I'll do what I can to help you get over this."

Chris felt like she could tell this man anything. He seemed so sincere and sweet. His big blue eyes were intent, and he looked like a young boy with his ruddy complexion and tousled light brown hair. She liked the feeling of him sitting near her. He was tall and looked strong. She felt safe.

Softly Chris replied. "Please don't feel so bad. It's my fault for waiting so long. I should have told you the truth to begin with. But, yes, yes, I do need to talk about it. I'm so glad you're here."

Chris proceeded to tell Spence about her entire Saturday and this Sunday morning. She talked and talked and, at times, cried. Spence listened intently and put his arm around Chris when she cried, realizing what traumatizing events she had just endured.

"…And then a policewoman took me home and here I am. If only I hadn't told a lie to begin with when Carla died, all this wouldn't have happened to Dawn and me. I'm so sorry and have been ever since then, but I was so scared to get my family involved because we've been through so much already. You just don't know."

"Why don't you tell me, Chris?"

"Are you sure? It's a long story."

"I'm sure. I want to know about your life and I have lots of time."

Then Chris relayed her life of the last year or so, not

leaving anything out. She talked and talked for a long time, and it felt so good talking to this man. Spence listened with interest.

After she had finished, Spence looked deeply into her eyes and said, "You are a very strong lady." He held her closer.

They sat together on the sofa with Wittles nestled on Chris' lap. Chris thought it was heavenly. She needed the closeness of Spence right now. She felt protected, a feeling she hadn't had in a long, long time.

All three of them were just about to doze off when they heard someone's stomach growl loudly. They both laughed trying to determine whose stomach was making the noise because they were sitting so close together.

"Excuse me, I think that was me." Spence said.

They laughed again.

"Why don't we order some food? I don't know about you but I could eat anything. I'm starved."

Then Spence's stomach growled even more loudly.

Chris and Spence giggled like little kids and Wittles ran from lap to lap just having fun.

Pizza, breadsticks, and salads were ordered along with soda pop from Mimi's Pizza. Chris had a bottle of wine in her car from Terry's store, but she would pour that down the sink and throw the bottle away. Spence was happy with ginger ale, so they ate around 10:00 when the food was delivered.

Spence left around midnight. He had to be at work at 6:30 the next morning. Chris decided to call in sick on Monday; she just couldn't leave her house just yet.

Spence said he would call when he could and giving Chris a big hug and Wittles a good belly rub, he left.

Chapter 72

The next morning the kids called and were excited about their vacation. They didn't seem to miss Chris and to be honest she was happy they weren't here. She needed the time to herself.

The week went by too quickly and Chris relished every day. When she came home after work, the house was clean and quiet. She would shower, put on comfortable clothes, take Wittles for a walk, and read. Dinner was either take out or something very simple.

Spence came over when he could, and they watched old movies and cuddled on the couch. Chris really enjoyed his company and was starting to like the guy immensely. He told her that Terry was in jail, waiting for a hearing and a mental evaluation. Eight of his fourteen cats had to be put to sleep because of diseases or infected wounds too far gone to heal. The other cats had been shaved, bathed, neutered, and given their shots. Hopefully, most of them would find foster homes until they could be adopted.

During one of their conversations, Spence told Chris that he had been married for four years and then divorced five years ago. There were no children, although he was crazy about kids. Chris was relieved.

Sunday came and sure enough her happy kids arrived around 3:00. They all looked so relaxed and tan, and Chris had to admit she was glad they were home.

Despite her enjoying the always clean, quiet house, she had missed them.

Chapter 73

The household settled back to normal, and everyone continued to enjoy what was left of the summer. Spence became a regular visitor, and Chris' children seemed to like him a lot. He was cheerful, funny, and attentive. The boys were very impressed that he was a detective. They all went on occasional picnics and outings on the weekends, sometimes with Laura and her family.

Chris and Spence also spent time just together, movies, dinners, long walks, but mostly they were all together at Chris' home.

It took Chris two weeks before she told Laura the whole story of that weekend. Laura was absolutely shocked to say the least and insisted on telling Don; it was quite the conversation between the grown-ups for a while.

Chapter 74

It was a gorgeous day, the sun shining, temperatures in the seventies. Cool for August, but just perfect after a spell of very hot weather. The air was clean and clear, and Chris opened all the windows and doors to take advantage of the gentle breeze. Life was good.

It was Saturday and this was supposed to be school shopping day, but Chris decided it was too pleasant to spend inside the mall. American Eagle and Forever 21 would have to wait another day. The kids were still sleeping, and Chris took her tea and Wittles out back for some rays of sun.

As she lay on the lounger, her face to the morning sun, she thought about what her life was like just one year ago. Thankful, so very thankful, it was over. What a year! Who would believe? She quieted her negative thoughts and willed herself to think about the good things to come. She smiled while her whole body relaxed.

Then the phone blared, "Damn it." Chris ran to get the phone before it woke the kids.

She grabbed the phone and begrudgingly answered, "Hello."

It took only "hi" and she realized who was on the other side of the line—of course, why not!

"Hello, Ted, what can I do for you?"

"Hey, Chris, as you must know, I've been out for over about a month now."

"No, I didn't know."

"Well, anyway, I have. I'm surprised Mr. Lyons didn't tell you. I've been staying in a rental house waiting for my friend to get out of jail, and we're planning a partnership of sorts down in Florida. He got out last week."

"That's nice," Chris said disinterestedly.

"Anyway, I want to get the car today and sell it because Lisa and I are moving to Florida this week."

"Okay, what time?"

"How about in an hour or so?"

"Sure."

"I know, of course, where to go, after all, it was MY home and the home of MY parents."

"Don't start anything, Ted, just get the car and go to Florida."

"You're right. I do want to say goodbye to the kids and uh, of course, you."

"Yeah sure, see you in an hour." Chris banged the receiver down. She was boiling mad. "Didn't think that jerk could bother me anymore, but I just let him ruin my beautiful day."

Chapter 75

Chis woke up the kids, telling them their father was coming to get the car. Scott was the only one that seemed interested.

"Come on, sleepyheads, your dad wants to say goodbye. He's going to Florida and he'll be here in an hour."

"Isn't that just wonderful," Becky said sarcastically as she got in the shower. Bobby and Scott got dressed and headed to the breakfast table.

Bobby said, "You know, Mom, I don't really care if I ever see Dad. Is that bad or what?"

"I guess you feel what you feel. There's no right or wrong about it. Just be polite. Maybe someday you'll feel differently."

"Maybe," he continued eating his cereal.

Scott said, "I want to see my dad. It's been a long time. If they let him out of jail that must mean he's not a bad guy anymore, right Mom?"

"Scott, your dad isn't a bad man, but he made a bad mistake. They let him out of jail because they don't think he'll do anything bad anymore."

"Okay, that makes sense."

Chapter 76

As he said, in one hour, Ted pulled up in a red Mercedes. By his side sat a girl Chris supposed was Lisa. "Oh great, this day gets better and better."

Ted and Lisa walked to the garage, and Lisa was introduced to Chris and the children. Scott hugged his father and the other two stood their distance.

Lisa gushed, "Oh, they are such beautiful children. The older boy looks just like you, Ted."

Chris sighed, "His name is Bobby."

Bobby shuffled back and forth and didn't say a word. Awkward, very awkward, that's all Chris could think. She couldn't believe Lisa didn't even know his name.

Chris gave Ted the keys and told him there were two boxes of toys and things she thought he might like. He looked in the boxes and said no thanks. Chris didn't press the issue.

Of course, after sitting in the garage for so many years, the car didn't start and Ted called AAA for a tow. An uncomfortable half hour followed.

"When we get to Florida, I'll give you my new address for emergencies and such." Ted said.

"Okay."

"Maybe the kids could come and visit sometimes when we get our house ready and see their new baby brother or sister," Lisa said with a smile.

Ted whispered, "Not now, Lisa," but she continued. "I'm not quite a month along but we're so happy to be having a baby. The girl would make a perfect babysitter. You do like babies, don't you, honey?"

"Her name is Becky," Chris said, absolutely appalled at Lisa's bad judgment.

The look in Becky's eyes gave Lisa the finger, and she turned and walked toward the house. She stopped abruptly and turned around. "We're happy now, Dad, why don't you and your girlfriend just go to Florida and leave us alone?" She then stomped into the house as only a sixteen-year-old girl can do.

"What did I say?" Lisa stammered.

Thankfully, the tow truck pulled up and attention was drawn to the process of loading the car.

Before Ted and Lisa left, Chris motioned for Ted to talk to her, away from the others. "When you do get a job, I hope you remember something called child support. You ARE their father, you know. I am going through Mr. Lyons on this, so you need to notify him of your address. Just because you are having a new child doesn't mean you can forget the three you already have."

"They hate me, Chris."

"Doesn't matter, you still have an obligation to them. And maybe, if you try real hard, write them letters, acknowledge their birthdays and holidays, have Lisa learn their names, maybe, just maybe you can be their father again. Everyone needs a father, and you haven't been there for them for a long time."

"I've been in prison."

"Yes, and you could have written, phoned, something—anything. But even before that you weren't available to any of us for a long time. If you want the privilege of being their father again, you need to, well, earn it back. And I'm not kidding about child support. We had it so very hard this last year. You need to step up."

Ted waved his hands. "Well, you've got all this now from my mother, what else do you want?"

"It was her choice, Ted. I had nothing to do with it."

"Yeah, right." He walked away.

"Take it to Bonds on Meadow Drive." Ted instructed the tow truck driver.

"Goodbye, boys, and tell Becky goodbye for me. I'll be calling soon and maybe you can enjoy sunny Florida this winter for a visit."

"That would be neat, Dad," Scott said, as he gave Ted a hug. Always, always hopeful Scott. Chris really did hope that some day all the kids would have a good relationship with their father.

The truck pulled the old car out. Ted and Lisa got in the Mercedes and they left.

Chris sighed with relief. It was over. She would hardly ever have to see him again. Maybe for weddings and such, but that would be a long time from now.

The boys went in the house and Chris went to close the garage door. She spotted the two boxes and decided they would be put on the curb come garbage day. She closed the garage door and was walking back to the house when a familiar car pulled up.

Spence got out of the car and walked towards Chris. He had a smile on his face and a pizza in his hands.

Chris' mood brightened immediately. The day was beautiful again. Life was good.

About the Author

Barbara Wood Polak is a native of Dayton, Ohio, and a graduate of Miami University in Ohio. She is a former elementary school teacher and resident of several other states. She is a wife, mother, grandmother, and soon-to-be great-grandmother. *Boomerang Lies* is her first novel.

The author's dog Cosette (Cosy) is the inspiration for Wittles, the fluffy, playful Bichon Frisé featured in *Boomerang Lies*.